Pieces of Chaos

Tommy B. Smith

A Black Diamond book.

Cover art by Drop Dead Designs.

First Rainstorm Press Edition: November 2013

Black Diamond Edition: September 2018

ISBN: 0692152121
ISBN-13: 978-0692152126

TABLE OF CONTENTS

Fragment: A Brief Note from the Author

So words are wasted and lost in time, it may sometimes seem, but time itself, and ink and paper, in any literal or figurative sense, may capture them from the drift.

On any given day, we walk out, or in, rather, into the great wide world, bouncing from situation to situation while faces float past us along the streets, each concealing a story we may never know behind strange visages we may never see again.

One such story is comprised of many, many smaller stories, and those stories are composed of...

I'll leave this to your imagination.

Perhaps we have stood face-to-face, and perhaps not, and if not, perhaps someday we will or, then again, perhaps we never will, but in these pages we share something unique.

Tommy B. Smith

March 2013

Patient #37

"You should have left me in the dark," she whispered as the light fell across her. "You should have left me in the dark!"

"It's time for—"

"Leave me alone," Cinnamon said, inching backward and pressing as deeply as she could into the padded wall just behind her.

"But Ms. Caraway, you haven't eaten in—"

"I don't need anything!" Cinnamon shouted. Her emaciated frame shifted and her large, bloodshot eyes stared holes through the apprehensive orderly and the food tray he held. "You bring that in here constantly, and it's a waste of time. It's terrible and teeming with bacteria, and you're only letting unfiltered air into my room every time you open the door!"

The orderly shook his head in surrender and set the tray down on the floor, then backed away. He knew that Cinnamon Caraway, if that was indeed even her real name, had never presented a danger to anyone but herself. For this reason, the food tray featured no eating utensils.

She tried to take her own life once before, and since that occurrence, no sharp objects were allowed to enter her room. The orderly remembered the day well, when the staff found her soaking quietly in a pool of her own blood, clutching the knife and fork in a white-knuckled grip and carving away at her flesh as though she meant to free herself from her own skin.

The orderly shut the door quietly, closing the lock, and he stole one last glance through the metal security door's small Plexiglas window. Cinnamon still sat with her back against the wall, staring with a steady gaze, her eyes unreadable.

Since Cinnamon had been confined to her protective cell in the mental hospital, she had refused to take any nourishment. They had investigated her background and came back with nothing. She had given her name as Cinnamon Caraway, but to the orderly, that didn't even sound like a real name.

The orderly nearly jumped out of his skin, roused from his thoughts to notice Cinnamon's face just on the other side of the window. She laughed, seeing she had frightened him, and licked

1

the Plexiglas. He turned to hurry away, now unnerved, and when he looked back, she had already disappeared from the window.

Cinnamon returned to her corner. Eventually she let out a yawn and lowered herself onto the cool floor. Her gaze turned to the food tray. She hated it with every fiber of her being.

She wanted only to transcend this life. She wanted no part of this diseased reality, its maddeningly ridiculous concepts, or the mockery that lingered in the air and upon the lips and eyes of every face. It was the cruelest of injustices to have been dealt the losing card from the beginning.

She also hated the open sky. The shield of her dark prison could not conceal it from her, nor her from it. It made her feel naked and vulnerable.

Outside, the orderly held his thoughts of that dark cell's interior at bay. He stared at the clock. It was nearly over. When the time arrived, the orderly shook his head a last time and left.

He glanced up to the sky, uneasy, before he climbed into his car and drove out of the parking lot. He turned up the radio and accelerated down the street. As he crossed the railroad tracks, his eyes wandered again to the green sky.

Beyond the walls of the compound, Cinnamon's eyes were closed, but the train's motion traced the back of her eyelids.

The vehicle disappeared with the crunch of tons of grinding metal. Sounds of the horrific crash and explosion reached her, even so deep inside the compound.

Her eyes blinked open and she stretched out on the floor of her cell. Feeling surrounded and outnumbered in the silence, she took solace in the truth that the joke of jokes was not on her.

The smallest cell and subatomic particle had been molded and shaped in eternal detail by the limitless focus of Chaos and Order, equals and opposites, boundaries which enveloped everything and nothing. She held the key to that structural formula of higher dimensions in her very mind. As it all had come into being, it could also be undone.

Cinnamon curled up in her corner, her head filled with despair, shame, and a multitude of other emotions which brought on the twisted dreams that plagued her every night. If only she had seen beyond the sum of it all, she would never have spun the fabric of this universe into existence.

Chronicle of the Golden Pyramid

To me, the world is dead. In the wake of my countless days and nights of hopeless reflection and despair, I withdrew from society and burned all of my physical possessions which reminded me of any connections I shared with others.

There was only me, the sparse interior of my destitute living space, and the mirror. I stared into the mirror, at first in disdain at the presence of my own unbecoming reflection, and then I managed to focus on the background image of the Pyramid interminably insinuated in the mirror's surface.

When I first traversed the steep, shimmering surface of the Pyramid at the age of forty-six, I didn't grasp its meaning. I didn't understand my role among the secrets of its mysterious majesty. Instead, for the first time since my childhood years, I was frightened.

The Pyramid is not one in the traditional sense as compared to the pyramids of Egypt. The historical pyramids were wonders of architecture in their own right, but they were constructed long ago upon the desert sands of Egypt, whereas the solitary Pyramid I refer to is of another nature altogether.

No, my Pyramid is a golden monument to something unnatural, and even alien, to this mundane world.

The Pyramid has no interior. It is a structure marked on its perfectly sloped outer shell by an uncanny network of connecting walkways and stairways.

When I first stood on the Pyramid, I was mystified. The sky above was the darkest black and blackness lay at the base of the Pyramid, for there is no ground to support the structure. It is imposed in the endless black nothingness which encases it.

I was afraid because the air was still and the intense quiet strangely uncomfortable. The feeling of isolation outweighed anything I had ever experienced. Though frightened, I also sensed a sadness, a loneliness, in my surroundings.

I was at least reassured by the nearby mirror leaning against one wall. Aside from my own reflection, it featured the outline of my Spartan bedroom in its surface.

3

I describe only my first moments on the Golden Pyramid. I later came to shed the strange fear and sadness, and changes began to overtake me. A profound desire possessed me, an obsession if you will, to reach the top of the Pyramid. It was there, I sensed, that I would find an answer to this conundrum. This became clear to me in the first instant that I heard her cries of wretched hopelessness.

In an effort to reach the Pyramid's summit, I made my way to the end of the first walkway and climbed the set of steps to the next level. I met a walkway featuring two similar sets of steps on each end, so I chose one at random and continued my ascent.

Once I had climbed a substantial portion of the Pyramid's myriad of stairways and balconies, I heard the feminine wailing from far above. She was clearly distressed beyond all reason, but of what, I could not fathom. What beast tormented her, what manner of monster I might be forced to confront atop the Pyramid, I could not imagine, but the yearning to unravel the Golden Pyramid's silent riddle pressed me onward in my persistent attempts to reach its peak.

The answer eluded me. I awoke on my cot in the familiar confines of my bedroom. I lay in disoriented contemplation of the Golden Pyramid for minutes until I finally stood and in a frustrated burst of fury, smashed my bedside lamp against the wall. Glass rained onto my hardwood floor. It crunched beneath my feet as I abruptly turned to approach the mirror.

The outline of the Pyramid remained there as always. The answers had not been mine on this day, but I vowed that one day, my efforts would see fruition. I would reach the top of the Golden Pyramid and the answers *would* be mine.

I concluded that the petty concerns and cares of the world were nothing more than a burden to me and to my purpose. My destiny awaited at the top of the Golden Pyramid.

I began taking sedatives on a regular basis and spent much of my time in slumber. I lived as a recluse, only venturing out of my home to purchase absolute necessities. I continued popping my pills like candy and staring into the mirror before I allowed myself to fall onto the cot.

I would find myself on the Golden Pyramid, standing near the mirror. In my increasingly frenzied rush to climb the Pyramid, I would strain to recall the quickest route to ascend its surface. Every time, I would wake before I could reach the Pyramid's upper region, her fading screams and sobs the last lingering trace of it in my mind as my failure was repeated.

I sat on the edge of my cot with my head in my hands until another desperate notion came to me. I would do anything possible to reach the top of the Pyramid, and because of this, I committed myself to my ultimate solution.

I proceeded through the rest of the day with more calm than I had mustered in the past year. I even went out into public and bought myself groceries. I prepared myself one of the finest meals I had eaten since I could remember. I had a glass of white table wine, and then I took a handful of sleeping pills. I looked at the mirror, and at the outline of the Pyramid, until the sedatives set in.

I stood on the Pyramid. I looked at the mirror, at the faint image of my bedroom lurking behind my reflection.

I lifted the mirror and with all of my strength, threw it against the wall of the Pyramid. It fractured in an explosion of silver fragments. I grabbed the mirror's frame and flung it from the Pyramid into the blackness below, where it vanished forever.

I climbed the Pyramid with slow deliberation and patience, unimpeded. I did not awaken in my bedroom, nor would I ever.

Her anguished cries grew more audible as I neared the top of the Pyramid. I reached the final golden set of stairs, a flight longer than any of the others, and this extended a great distance upward toward my destination at the Pyramid's summit.

As I set foot upon the top of the Golden Pyramid, she cried out, "Do not look upon me! You will seal my end!"

Her words were for naught. The sight met my eyes, even after she had warned me.

Chains bound her to a gigantic clock, one featuring no hands to mark the hours and minutes. She was naked and her fragile beauty was exposed in full.

The winding paths of fate came together and her purpose became known to me, as did my own.

I knew the essence of the beast, the horror of which she had existed in perpetual fear. I knew the terrible thing that obsessed to reach her at the Pyramid's pinnacle, the monstrosity that could not be denied in its own dominion, and as I moved toward her I knew that, at the highest point of the forlorn Golden Pyramid, no one would hear her final screams.

Epitaph for Sol

As the wrath of Heaven's might seemed flung down upon them, the inhabitants of Sol were swept up in the Dance of Death. Wild and raving were those afflicted, extremities burning and bodies covered with parasites driven of divine judgment, microscopic beasts with a hunger so determined that every blemish of purity became a morsel of rapt delicacy.

Those caught in the harshest rigors of the holy torment were burned throughout by an inner fire, its intensity so great that it might have consumed their souls during the final moments. Those with the luxury of a quick means to die launched themselves from the highest windows to the compassion of the ground far below. Death was the salvation of Sol, and for those who would live, peace of mind would remain ever the fleeting illusion.

The New Faith came to Sol, its zealots baptized in the fire of its wicked absurdities. In answer, the crimson dragon of righteousness descended to devour what remained of the condemned village.

The town's only place of worship burned, dispensed to its grim sentence by those who writhed in the torturous madness of the searing heavenly light. They had lost their will to the demons and reveled in the destruction of this renounced spiritual icon.

Father Hamund watched it burn. Even as he clung to his faith and his belief that mankind could defy its own monstrosity through the boundless guidance of the written word, his somber eyes reflected the fires. His face was weary, lined with age and grief. Sol was destroying itself. Sol wanted to die.

Quickly after the village's yearly Festival of Grace, the demons had come to Sol. They had named their favorites. The rest were devoured as the demons began their wicked feast and dined on those who lacked the strength to defy their yawning appetites.

For the wives with child, a horrific spell was unleashed, pushing them into the pains of immediate childbirth. The forced offspring, thought a product of the blackest phantoms, were gathered by those taken by demonic influence or consumed by holy vengeance. Father Hamund dared not contemplate their fates.

Gontier, one of the village elders, claimed his seat as the harbinger of the New Faith. As prime subject of the forces that governed the undoing of Sol, Gontier directed his maniacal enthusiasts to burn the holy place and committed himself to the eradication of the enduring righteous.

Father Hamund had the protection of his faith. Untouched, he watched the flames engulf every ember of Sol's simple lone cathedral until a new scream pierced his veil of sadness.

"Leave me be!" a child wailed as they dragged him toward the blazing cathedral. Two men of the New Faith pulled him along, one by each arm, under the supervision of Gontier. They laughed at his vain struggles.

"Into the glare!" the men shouted in gleeful unison. "Into the glare! Into the glare!" The horrified child screeched in terror. He struggled and pleaded, but his captors continued to drag him toward the impending flames.

"No!" he screamed as they lifted him from his feet, preparing to hurl him into the fire.

"Unhand the boy!" Father Hamund roared. He charged. The men received his advance with eyes glazed by madness. Gontier crossed his arms. His demeanor scarcely masked his growing excitement.

"He received the boy with great happiness," Gontier spoke in an authoritative tone, as if reciting a passage in some perverse religious service. "And His will was then fed by a speaker of divine falsehoods and this brought Him and His beloved everlasting joy!"

Father Hamund threw himself forward. His body connected with one of the men. The action came a moment too late.

Hurled at the same instant, the boy landed just outside the fire's reach. The heat singed his flesh as he stumbled. Hamund's heart skipped a beat. While the man he had struck tumbled to the ground in surprise, other man pulled a knife from his belt.

Father Hamund lunged to seize the boy's wrist and yanked him backward to safety. The boy cried out a warning. Father Hamund turned as the knife came forth. He gasped as it gashed his shoulder. The two men grappled and Father Hamund twisted the knife from his attacker's grip. With his assailant disarmed, he backed away. Blood soaked the clothing near his wound. While it was not a critical injury, the pain in his shoulder was sharp.

Gontier babbled with insistence that the men should kill both Father Hamund and the boy without hesitation. Father Hamund threw his uninjured arm around the boy and hauled him away from the scene faster than the child's small legs could carry him.

Someone heaved and vomited nearby while another spasmed uncontrollably on the ground. Father Hamund ran past them with a final look to the dying cathedral.

In Sol, there was no one left to save. Drawing the young boy along with him, Hamund fled the doomed village.

It was night when the two slowed their trek from Sol. The panic still haunted the boy's eyes, but obvious fatigue now dulled his senses. Father Hamund attempted to make conversation, if only to keep the boy alert to continue their retreat.

"What is your name?"

The boy flinched at the sudden question. He swallowed and said nothing for a time, but then turned his ashen face to Hamund.

"Arnaud," the boy replied. Father Hamund could hear the reluctance in his quiet voice and did not press him further. The boy had seen too much pain for one so young.

"I will see to it that you are safe," Hamund spoke.

They said nothing else for the remainder of their journey into the night until they stopped to rest and take a meal. Father Hamund, though nagged by an unshakable paranoia, deduced the likelihood that Gontier had not pursued them in their journey, nor had any of the others seized by the infernal persuasions of the New Faith.

Father Hamund produced the bread and cheese from his pack and offered the larger portion to the boy, who was thin and from an apparent impoverished upbringing. The boy thanked Father Hamund, but declined.

After several more fruitless attempts to share his fare with young Arnaud, Father Hamund ate alone. It was a light meal, but the cheese and rye bread would keep his hunger away for now.

An undeterminable span of time later into the night, during the darkest hours, Father Hamund felt the Devil's madness creeping into him. The fire began to overtake him.

He spent the late hour in prayer, but with every sincere word uttered, the fire only grew in its insistence.

He looked to Arnaud, who lay in peaceful slumber a distance away. Father Hamund took out the knife he had wrested from one of Gontier's men in Sol, the one who had wounded him.

The fire burned with unrelenting vigilance. Father Hamund was losing himself to the demons' terrible whims, and once this was done, the boy's well-being, both physical and spiritual, would be at risk.

Questions of salvation weighed on Father Hamund's ailing mind. He turned the knife over in his wrinkled hands. A tear spilled down his cheek. He looked up to the starry heavens and pressed the knife against his wrist.

"Father, please forgive me for what I must do," he whispered.

* * *

In the Middle Ages, the affliction known as Saint Anthony's Fire raged periodically through Europe. By the year 1676, a scientific discovery by Denis Dodart revealed the nature of Saint Anthony's Fire, also known as the Holy Fire, to be a product of ergot poisoning due to the consumption of contaminated rye bread. This phenomenon is also speculated to have been responsible for the hysteria that manifested in Salem, Massachusetts in 1692.

Electric Presence

The scream from the phone's receiver struck John's senses like a hammer to the skull. The bedside alarm clock blared. The lights in the house flickered. In the next instant, the radio fell silent, the house went dark again, and a dial tone bleated from the phone's receiver.

On that first starless Saturday night, the presence came into their lives. Even into the following night, a sense of vulnerability lingered. They tried to drive it from their thoughts, but Alicia tossed in her sleep until she woke and blinked at the illumination. She shook her husband awake.

"You left the living room light on."

"I did?" John murmured. "I could swear I turned it off." He rubbed his eyes and looked toward the bedroom door. Light shone from beneath the crack at its base. He stood from the bed and walked sleepily to the living room. He squinted to adjust. The light was on, but the switch was in the *off* position. Bewildered, John flicked the switch back and forth a few times. The light remained on.

At this hour, nothing else could be done about it. He returned to bed. "It must be some kind of electrical problem," he said to Alicia.

After a restless night, John managed to drag himself out of bed, take a shower, and fall into his work clothes. The living room light was off now, he noticed.

Whatever the problem was, he would have to take a look at it later, when he had the time. The incident from Saturday night lingered in his hazy, tired mind, however: that insane phone call, when the entire house had seemed to go crazy.

But it was just a house. Houses can't go crazy, because they're just houses.

At lunch, John sat at a break room table eating the turkey sandwich Alicia had packed for him.

"How's the new place?" Tony asked.

"It leaves a lot to be desired," John replied, "at least compared to our old house. It'll do, though, until I can get back on my feet." Tony nodded. John decided not to mention anything about the disturbances in the house.

"That's crazy talk," Tony would inevitably say.

Tony didn't seem much for conversation today anyway, so there was no point in pestering him about it. John focused instead on finishing the half-eaten turkey sandwich in front of him.

"How was work?" Alicia asked John later, over supper.

"Not bad," John responded absently between bites of spaghetti.

"Things will get better for us," Alicia assured him. "Just give it time."

"Maybe," John said. He picked up a piece of garlic bread.

Alicia did what she could to bolster her husband's failing confidence, but reality was reality. Things hadn't been the same since the business crashed, forcing John into a job he didn't relish in order to make ends meet.

At least they still had their health, though, and their marriage.

"How's Tony?" Alicia asked.

"He wasn't talking much today," John answered.

"He's got a lot on his mind, I'm sure," Alicia said. "Did he and Emily ever patch things up?"

"I don't know," John said. "He didn't mention it, but he knows we have our own problems. I'm sure he's just dealing with it the best way he can."

After supper, and an hour of channel surfing, John decided to retire to bed early. Though the house still made him uncomfortable and the odd sensation of apprehension remained, he was able to dismiss the troubling memory of the previous nights. With the aid of the day's fatigue, he drifted into a restful sleep.

He woke to an eerie feeling. He looked over to see Alicia was already awake, staring back at him.

"What's wrong?" John asked.

"I don't know," she whispered. She climbed out of bed, pushed a curtain aside, and looked out the bedroom window. "Something's—"

The alarm clock's clamor cut Alicia short. John sat up rigidly. Alicia tried to switch off the alarm clock, but the blaring continued until she unplugged it. John looked toward the door and saw the trace of light shining beneath it.

The living room light had come on again. He went to turn it off again, unsuccessfully, just as before.

"I don't like this," Alicia said when he returned, unmistakable tension in her voice. "What's happening?"

"I don't know." John took a deep breath. "But whatever it is, it isn't going away. I'll look into it tomorrow. Let's try to get some sleep for now."

* * *

The following day at work, Tony seemed to be in a better mood. John couldn't get the recent occurrences in the new house out of his mind, so he decided to mention it to his friend and co-worker.

"Have you ever heard anything about that house on North Oak that Alicia and I moved into?" he asked.

"Not a lot," Tony said. "Some older couple lived in it before you did, I think. Why?"

"What happened to them?"

"The husband passed away," Tony recounted. "I think the widow ended up in a nursing home. Where's this going?"

"We've had some—" John began, but faltered as he grasped for some way to explain it. "We've had some *things* happening since we've moved in."

"What kinds of things?" Tony asked.

"Lights coming on, for one. And Alicia and I both woke up late last night when the alarm clock went off."

"That's not so strange," Tony said. "You probably set it for the wrong time."

"I *know* I didn't. This isn't the first time this has happened, either. It all started last Saturday night."

"I wouldn't give it too much thought, John." Tony downed the last of his sack lunch and leaned back in his seat. "You've had a lot going on with the move and starting this new job. All that stress is probably getting to you. You might want to have the light switch looked at, but other than that, I'm sure there's a logical reason for all of it. Electrical problems, maybe."

"You're probably right," John said. "But until we can put it all together, I don't think I'll be able to get over it. I've heard all the weird stories you can imagine, but I've never actually had things like this happen to me before. Alicia and I have both been stressed out lately." He sighed. "So what about you, Tony? Are you and Emily all right?"

"We're fine," Tony said. "We had a talk the other night and worked everything out. Listen, John, back to what we were talking about before, if you want my advice, after you get off work today, just go home and relax. Maybe go to bed early. I'm sure this will all pass."

* * *

"Honey!" Alicia whispered at one-thirty-eight in the morning. She shook her husband to wake him.

"What is it?" John asked. He sat up, startled, and attempted to gather his wits. Noises were coming from the living room, voices. Someone was in the living room!

John sprang to his feet. The living room light was on again. He prepared himself for conflict. He opened the bedroom door, crept toward the living room, and peered around the frame of the doorway.

He saw no one in the living room, but the television was on and it blasted at a ridiculous volume. The voices, still babbling, had come from the television program.

John silenced it by yanking the television's cord out of the outlet. He resolved to get some sleep, no matter what, and headed for the house's circuit panel. He switched off the main breaker, shutting down the power to the entire house.

The air became cold, an instant transition.

John tried returning to bed, but sleep became impossible. The chill increased. When John returned to the living room, he saw something that shocked him beyond words.

The front door stood wide open.

He looked outside and scanned the surrounding area. He saw no one anywhere around. The outside night air was cool. The chill stemmed from inside the house.

As John closed the door and locked it, dread began to gnaw at him.

It was freezing cold now. John shivered. What was going on? What had he done in shutting off the house's electricity? He couldn't take much more of it. He switched the house's main circuit back on, restoring power. Immediately, the phone rang.

John gasped. Alicia entered the living room in her night gown. Her widened eyes locked John in a meaningful stare. She moved to answer the phone.

"Wait," John said.

He meant to allow the phone to ring long enough for the caller ID to pinpoint the number this time, but after one ring, it desisted, leaving no visible record of the call.

At least the cold had begun to abate. Alicia dropped onto the couch.

"I don't think I'll be able to go back to sleep," she said. John silently agreed and sat down beside her. They were in for a long night.

* * *

"I'm telling you, something's going on inside that house," John insisted.

"That's crazy talk," Tony said. He rubbed his whiskered chin.

"You still believe there's a logical explanation? Explain it to me."

"If you want, I could come over and stay the night," Tony said. "Just to throw that out there. I could stay on the couch and see what happens for myself."

"You think you could make some kind of warped sense out of this?"

"Who knows? I could try. If things are like you say, it couldn't hurt to have another perspective on it. If anything happens again, I'll be around to see it firsthand."

"You would do that?" John asked. "What about Emily? Are you sure she'll be all right with staying a night at home by herself?"

"You don't have room for both of us over there, do you? Don't worry about it. She'll be fine."

"All right, then," John said. "I'll mention it to Alicia, and I'll give you a call later."

Once John was off work, back at home, and out of a hot shower, he brought up the day's conversation to Alicia.

Alicia had grown more uncomfortable within the new house every day. She agreed it would be a welcome change to have a friend stay over and have a third witness to the strange events, if they should happen again. She started supper for the three of them while John called Tony.

"I'm just glad to finally get out of that house," Tony later admitted over a supper of rosemary chicken, rice pilaf, and steamed vegetables.

"I thought you and Emily worked things out," John said. He sliced into a juicy, seasoned chicken breast.

"That's right," Tony said. He poked at his food with his fork. "But things aren't the same with us anymore."

"John and I don't always agree on everything," Alicia said across the table, "but we manage to work things out. Give it time."

"Maybe you're right," Tony said, but a trace of dejection remained in his voice.

"Are you going to be okay?" Alicia asked him.

"I think I'm just tired," he muttered.

"Are you sure you're up for this tonight?" John asked.

"It'll be fine."

After supper and a few listless, vegetative hours of television, the three turned in for the night. John set some blankets and a pillow on the couch before he and Alicia withdrew to the bedroom.

John remained awake for some time in anticipation of what might happen. He looked over to Alicia and saw she was having trouble sleeping as well. Eventually, John closed his eyes. He was on the brink of sleep when Alicia bolted upright in bed.

Her fearful eyes turned to John. John sat up. He opened his mouth to speak, but the phone's sharp ring cut him off.

The living room light had come on again. John hurried to the bedroom door and moved into the living room. Tony slept on the couch under a blanket, unaware.

The living room light flickered. The phone continued to ring. John answered it. From it, a female voice sobbed.

"Who is this?" John demanded, but a trace of fear cracked his voice. No answer came. A click brought the call to an end.

He looked at the caller ID. This time, a number appeared, Tony's number.

"What?" John breathed, aghast. He looked again to Tony's sleeping form. After a moment's confusion, he grabbed his car keys and headed for the front door.

"Where are you going?" Alicia asked, a distance behind.

"I'll be back. I have to find out what's going on." John rushed out the door, unable to hear her reply, and jumped into the car. He started it and took off, speeding toward Tony's house.

The house was dark. John pulled into the driveway and killed the engine. He walked to the front door and knocked.

"Emily?" he called. "Are you there?" He knocked a second time, and again, no one answered. John backed up a few steps, and charged forward. He threw his shoulder heavily against the wooden door. With a loud crack, it gave way, and John tumbled into the interior.

An unusual smell assaulted his nostrils. The home smelled of decay and death. With mounting tension, John made his way through the house until he reached the bathroom.

Emily's body lay submerged in the bathtub's stale water. An electric toaster accompanied her in the tub, its cord drawn tight and plugged into a wall outlet.

Everything became a blur. John fell into tears, sickened and upset outside of reason. He scrambled to find the telephone and call the authorities.

For weeks, John struggled to sort it out in his mind. Only weeks later, when he and Alicia drove away from that home on North Oak for the last time, did he manage between the account of the police investigation and what his own eyes had witnessed.

From the extent of the decomposition, Emily had been dead for days. The neighbors spoke of screams and terrible fighting next door on that clouded, starless Saturday night before Tony and Emily's house went silent.

Tony, the prime suspect in the case, would be confirmed as his wife's murderer, but he would never stand trial. He had died that night on John and Alicia's couch, his heart stopped by a powerful current which could only have come from the electric heating blanket that covered him.

Alligator Death Roll

The place buzzed like a raucous beehive with all of the charm. In the corner, the guffaw and roar of "pour me another one, laddie!" caused Salvadore Shaw to sigh and rub his temples when he passed. He resolved to have a drink the instant he found his seat in this dump.

His empty seat awaited right across from a dark, skinny fellow who helped himself to an unidentified mass of grease and cholesterol. When he slid into the chair, the young man looked up from the last bite of the meal that soaked the paper-lined basket in front of him and asked, "You Sal Shaw?"

Without answering his question, Salvadore Shaw asked in turn, "Are you Ira?"

"Yeah," the other man said with a suppressed grin that glinted of gold teeth. Ira caught the girl as she passed by their table and ordered a sloe gin fizz.

As for Sal, "Johnnie Black, neat."

The girl disappeared to retrieve their order. Ira placed a toothpick in his mouth and leaned back in his chair. He chewed the toothpick and studied Sal in quiet, from his bronzy bald head to the white shirt and navy blue vest that adorned his bulk.

Much of the bulk was muscle, but not all. Over the years, Sal had shifted to making more trips to the bar and fewer visits to the gym, but his resume was sound. He had come out of his last job, something in the Northwest Territories of Canada, fairly well-to-do. Afterward, for the past year or so, he had dropped out of sight, but through some as-yet unsevered connection he had received word of the Jacobsen affair. Now he was here, of all places, ordering a scotch in a noisy shack in the middle of swamp country.

The drinks arrived. Ira reached up to remove the toothpick from the corner of his mouth.

"So you got a tip-off," he said at last. "Who's to say it ain't like all the other crazy stories flying around, and by that I mean the ones that ain't got a grain of truth to them?"

"It's a little more than a 'tip-off' and I think you know that," Sal said. "This isn't some tail-chasing shadow hunt." Sal slid his drink closer. He lifted the glass, inspected it, and took a sip. "Plus, I suspect some others may be interested in this little venture. I just need you to make sure I get there quick and I get there *first.*"

"Long as our little arrangement's still on," Ira said.

"It's on."

"No point in wasting time around this joint, then," Ira said. He held up his drink, extra-red and swirling with ice. "When I'm done, we'll head out."

Ira turned the glass up and gulped it down. Sal sacrificed his habit of microscopic sipping and finished his own drink. They both stood. Sal spilled some bills and change onto the table and walked toward the door. Ira followed. A quarter rolled across the abandoned table and dropped to the floor.

Outside, the rain had diminished to a thin mist. Sal hopped into the mud-spattered semi-white pickup truck parked out front and threw the passenger's side door open for Ira to climb in. Before Ira could shut the door, Sal backed up. He turned the wheel, and in seconds, they accelerated up the road. There was only one stop sign along the way, a four-way stop. Seeing no one else around, Sal ran it.

He turned the truck onto a lesser-traveled dirt—or mud, as the case was today—road and ground his foot into the gas pedal. The brown slime-sludge road narrowed and curved. Sal made no effort to slow.

"Watch out," Ira said.

Sal's eyes stayed ahead. "No worries. This thing's got good tires."

It didn't, but Sal knew there wasn't time to waste. They passed an even less-traveled road, more of a trail than a road. Neither of the men could see anything but tall, dirty grass in every direction.

"That's it, up ahead," Ira said.

"I see it," Sal replied. He pumped the brakes a few times and turned the wheel to slide the truck around in a queasy ninety-degree motion to redirect them along the new route, another trail, which lasted until the muddy bank and pier came into view.

Sal slowed. Beside the pier, a dark shape floated on almost-as-dark water, a boat.

"See it now?" Ira asked. Sal nodded once. He tried slowing the truck to a stop. Even after he braked fully, the wheels slid in the mud.

Ira jumped out and walked for the pier. Within half of a minute, Sal started after him.

Down by the pier, Ira climbed into the sleek ebony motorboat and revved the motor. Sal raked huge clumps of mud from his boots against the side of the pier before climbing in. He pulled a crumpled map from one pocket, unfolded it, and showed it to Ira.

Ira squinted at the map. "You sure this is right?" he asked.

"Is there a problem?" Sal replied.

Ira gave a shrug, and after another quick study of the map, shook his head. "I guess not."

"My sources say you know the area pretty well."

"It's just, the place we're supposed to be going—not an easy place to get to, and far as I know, there ain't nothing out there, either. No problem, though. I can get us there."

Sal folded the map to slide it back into his pocket. Ira walked to the front of the boat and turned to give a wave of some confusing kind which apparently meant "full speed ahead" because a second later, he threw the boat across the waters. Startled by the sudden jolt, Sal took a seat almost by accident.

The boat skimmed across scummy brown water. Foul droplets speckled Sal. He did his best to ignore it. Ira's speedboat flew unhindered beneath and around trees and past sludge-immersed foliage. At the front of the boat, Ira's head whipped around with his constant scanning of the horizon.

When the other boat appeared, Ira looked back at Sal, his eyes wide open. Sal said nothing. It was doubtful Ira could even hear him. It wasn't the time for words, anyway. Their peace had ended, Sal sensed. His hand closed around the Beretta in his jacket.

They could see two figures aboard the other boat, a man and a woman, both dark-featured. The man made a hand motion and shouted something. The woman who drove the boat glanced their way and quickly returned her focus to the waters ahead. The man raised a rifle.

Adrenaline took its hold. Sal yanked out the pistol and fired. A miss!

A flash issued from the rifle's barrel and a disconcerting thud told Sal and Ira their boat had been hit. Ira cursed and cut the boat to the right and then the left, while Sal took aim for another shot. Because of the wind and their erratic course, not to mention the distance, it was difficult to get a decent shot.

Just as he took careful aim and squeezed another shot, the boat bounced. Sal tumbled backward and collapsed into the back of the boat. Brown water rained down on him. His tailbone throbbed, but he braced himself when Ira swerved again. Another rifle shot plunked a hole through the frame of the boat. With a dismal pounding in his chest, Sal sat up and took aim again.

He had already missed twice. He might not have many more chances, if any. It was a tricky shot, flying around on the water like this with an enemy who did the same while knowing the rifleman's next bullet might be the one with Salvadore Shaw's name on it.

Sal fired. The rifleman went down, but this wasn't over.

He raised his gun to pick off the female driver of the boat, but she immediately turned her boat to speed away. Sal fired again but couldn't tell that it produced any result, and soon a tremendous distance separated the two boats, making it too difficult to train an accurate shot on her.

"We've been hit," Ira called, "but I think we're still good. Who was that?"

"No one I recognize," Sal said, "but they could be tied in with anybody." He tucked the Beretta under one arm and pulled out the map again. "According to this, she's headed the way we ought to be headed."

Ira craned his head to look back at Sal.

"Yes," Sal added, "we need to follow her."

Ira spurred the boat in pursuit. Sal nearly toppled again, but caught his balance and fired, "You need to warn me before you do that!"

The other boat wove rapidly between gnarled trees that jutted from the murk. Ira kept his eyes on the waters ahead. He steered the boat with precision to navigate what soon became a maze of obstacles and what might have been, for a lesser-skilled individual, eventual head-on impact.

The other boat had disappeared around a small foliage-rich mass of land, a miniature island in the brown water. Once they drew nearer to it, Ira cut the wheel to steer the boat around the tiny island and across open, deeper waters. The other boat was nowhere in sight.

Ira looked back to Sal, who shrugged. For the next few minutes, there were no further signs of the boat they had encountered. This made Sal uneasy, but he also knew they were coming closer to their goal as indicated by the map.

Sal wouldn't have expected the water could get any dirtier until he saw it for himself. A pall of shadows from clustered treetops soon fell over them. Another strange detail caught their notice, a multitude of protrusions from the swampy water's surface. Ira navigated the boat between these.

Sal leaned over the side to peer at them more closely. He balked, backing away from the side of the boat with his gun in his hand.

They were alligators, more of them than either of the men could count.

"They're everywhere," Ira breathed. "Man, I knew there were gators around here, but I ain't seen nothing like this before."

Sal didn't reply. He remained on edge, with a firm grip on his pistol.

Ira pushed the boat onward. The alligators continued to watch them from the water. Sal continued to watch them in kind. Ira kept looking ahead until he spotted the outline of a small cabin in the distance.

Ira held his hand over his eyes, more out of habit than necessity with such little sunlight here. "That it?" he asked.

Sal pried himself away from his vigilant alligator watch long enough to assess the cabin ahead. He nodded. Ira brought the boat in.

"Never knew this was out here," Ira murmured. "This day's just full of little surprises, ain't it?"

When the cabin came into clearer view, Ira brought the boat to a crawl. Wooden planks supported the cabin above the water.

The cabin itself was unevenly constructed and on the brink of falling apart. It appeared to have been haphazardly nailed together by the world's most inept builder. It had no windows, but it had a front door, and from it emerged an old man in khaki shorts and sandals with bony protruding knees and a long, white beard that swayed in front of a bulging stomach.

He jumped up and down, waving. "Saved!" he cried. "I'm saved, finally!"

Ira edged the boat closer. The motor sputtered and threw fumes into the air. The old man leaned forward, bushy eyebrows raised, to examine Ira and Sal once they came closer.

"You will give me a ride, won't you?" he asked.

Neither of the other men answered. Ira pulled the boat in and climbed out to tie a line to the single wooden post at a corner of the cabin's stand. Sal climbed out of the boat on the front end, following Ira.

Sal's gun remained in his hand. The old man seemed harmless, and Sal couldn't see any weapons on him, but he reasoned that one couldn't be too careful. The old man clearly saw the gun, but made no remark about it.

"Who are you?" Sal asked the man while Ira tied the boat's line.

"The name's Taggart," he said. He glanced at Sal's gun. "Did York send you two? Or was it Landry?"

Sal paused. "Neither," he said.

Taggart nodded. "Good," he said. "About that ride..."

"We'll talk," Sal said. "But first, we have a few questions of our own."

Ira finished securing the line and stepped back against the face of the cabin. Sal crossed the wooden planks.

"How did you get out here," Sal asked Taggart, "if you don't have any way back?"

"An associate of mine, I guess you might say," Taggart said. "We took his rowboat out here. What a mistake *that* was."

"What happened to the boat?"

Taggart motioned toward the dirty water. Sal and Ira looked, but saw nothing other than the brown liquid and, disconcertingly, several alligator heads watching them from its surface.

"That's right," Taggart said. "They got him."

"The alligators?"

"Yep."

"I asked about the boat." When no answer came, Sal met Taggart's meaningful stare. "You don't mean to tell me the alligators ate the whole boat, do you?"

"No, no," Taggart hastily replied. "The boat went down. But those evil critters might as well have swallowed it down chunk-by-chunk. Look at them out there, watching me! They've been circling this place since I got stranded here."

Sal shook his head. They didn't have time for this. They needed to hurry and find out what they could about—

"The gold," Taggart said. "That's why you two are here, I'm guessing."

For Sal, Taggart had spoken the magic words. "Where is it?" Sal asked.

"Right inside!" Taggart replied. "I'll show you."

That was easy enough, Sal thought, and along with Ira, he followed Taggart into the cabin. The inside of it was every bit of what he had expected after seeing the outside. He wasn't sure he felt safe standing here. It appeared as if the cabin might collapse at any second. He thought he could hear the boards groaning around him.

Taggart stepped past a single sleeping bag on the dirty floor to where a hefty burlap bag lay. He opened it wide. Sal and Ira leaned forward. Sal drew an audible breath while Ira stared with round eyes and appeared as if he might start drooling.

Stamped gold bars filled the bag, along with golden coins, large and small—a lot of them.

"Yes, sir," Taggart said. "Pure gold bullion, the real deal. Stashed back in the Depression days, wouldn't you know? Why Jacobsen didn't reclaim it over all those years, I may never guess, but he let the word of it slip on his deathbed, and well, Jacobsen had a lot of friends. I figured I'd better get out here before anyone else does. I guess you two had the same thinking."

"When a golden opportunity comes up," Sal said, "news travels fast."

Taggart cleared his throat. "Problem is, since I got here, I've been sitting around starving and watching those mean-looking gators run circles around this place. I guess they're starving too. You don't happen to have any food, do you?"

"There's some in my bag," Sal said. "Out in the boat."

"Mind if I get a bite to eat?" Taggart asked. "Being as I plan on splitting this here gold with you two for saving me. That's only fair, right? It don't do any good to have all the gold in the world if I'm stranded here."

Sal and Ira exchanged glances. Splitting the gold three ways had not been part of the initial plan. Ira's expression said to Sal, *what are you gonna do about this?* To which Sal's helpless shrug answered, *I don't know!*

Sal could always point his gun at Taggart and blast the old man into eternity, he knew, but could he bring himself to perform such a brutal act? He had killed before, sure, when he had to. He had shot a man just earlier, in fact, but that man had been armed, a threat. Sal had never gunned down an unarmed man in the cold-blooded fashion he had just considered.

Sal sighed. "Okay," he said. "Let's load the gold into the boat and get out of here."

"I'm with you all the way," old Taggart said. He stooped to lift the bag of gold, grunted, repositioned his legs, and heaved again to pull the heavy bag up into both arms.

"Got it," he said amid gasps. He stumbled out of the cabin between Sal and Ira. Sal climbed across the front of the boat and an unsteady Taggart transferred the large bag to Sal's arms. Sal took care in stepping backward to set the gold into the bottom of the boat.

Taggart jumped into the boat. Sal pulled a can of sardines from his satchel and threw it to the old man, who caught it at the side of the boat with a start, backing quickly from the edge with his eyes locked on the alligators that weren't far enough away for his comfort.

"The sooner we get out of here, the better," Taggart muttered.

Ira untied the line. "All set," he said. He stepped onto the boat, started the motor, and turned the boat around to speed away, leaving a wake of churning, frothy dark water.

Taggart stood up. "Ha!" he shouted at the numerous alligator heads glowering at him from the water. "Chew on this!" Taggart grabbed the front of his pants.

As Taggart sat back down to eat his can of sardines, Sal and Ira saw a familiar boat come into view.

Ira tensed. Sal went for his gun. Taggart dropped a sardine into his lap.

The female driver sped toward them. By the time Sal had his gun raised, her own gun was in her hand, and she took quick aim. Sal saw a flash. Ira screamed and tumbled backward past him.

Sal leveled his pistol and fired back. The woman's frame jerked and she went over the side of her boat.

Sal leaped to the wheel to direct the boat from the path of the other, now-unattended boat. A shape rose from the water. Sal recognized the woman's dark, wet hair plastered around her narrow feminine features.

Her arm raised from the water, pistol gripped in her hand. She aimed at Sal. He ducked low in the boat for cover, turned the boat toward her, and gunned the motor at full-speed.

The noise, incredible splashing interspersed with screaming, was audible even over the loudness of the boat's motor. Sal raised his head on impulse, immediately hoping it wasn't a mistake to do so, and his mouth fell open at the sight of the flopping, bloody spinning mass of meat.

The woman thrashed and wailed, rolling around in the alligator's clutches. Another alligator surged from one side to snap a second pair of jaws down on her. The two fought to rip her to pieces.

The boat flew toward the spinning feast. It was too late to stop. Sal braced himself for impact. A great slamming thump careened the boat upward. Sal clung to the wheel for all he was worth.

In the back of the boat, Ira clutched his bloodied arm. He lashed a hand out to grab one side of the boat. Taggart went flying, along with the bag of gold. Ira and Taggart shouted, both for different reasons. Ira flung out his only free arm.

With an immense splash, the boat dipped, crashing through dirty water to drench Sal in a dark cascade. He turned his dripping features back to see Ira lying in the back of the boat, bleeding from the bullet hole in his arm and trembling with fear. He clutched the bag of gold with both arms. Taggart was gone.

"I could only save one of them," Ira whispered. He squeezed the bag of gold.

Sal exhaled in relief. "Good move," he said.

He looked back to the boat's wake, where Taggart had gone into the water. From the rust-colored murk, an alligator head rose with a grotesque chunk of meat hanging from its mouth.

Sal gave a shake of his head. "We've got what we came for," he said. "Let's get out of this hellhole."

Mechanized

It is with great pride that I, Tetsuo Miyamoto, shall begin my journal dedicated to this most exciting opportunity to become a part of something of unquestionable magnitude: a glorious future.
In these corridors, machines are built, designed to think and work great tasks. The focus of the project known as M-2 is no mere robotic engineering; this is the creation and cultivation of artificial intelligence, a field of work which brings new advancements and startling discoveries with every turn.
The work I have poured into M-2 has been of exceptional value, to myself and the collective cause we all strive to perfect. This is a worthy pursuit for someone of my ability, and I feel it is a cause I can truly pour my life's work into without regrets.

Year One, November, Day Twelve

My work is my life. My mind is often occupied with details relating to my work with M-2. My superiors have assured me that my contributions are invaluable to the continued success of the project. The capabilities of our equipment are nearly endless, and in time, I believe we will carry the world into a new age.
These are not sentient beings with which we work. They are mere machines. Robotics and artificial intelligence could never supplant real people. The intricacy of these artificial life forms and their programming is amazing, nonetheless. "Drones" are the label we have given them, and they are many and varied.
We are opening a gateway to a new landmark in history which will change the world in ways unimaginable. Few know of this project and even fewer understand its potential, but I feel it is the beginning of something great.

Year Two, September, Day Four

The assistance of the new advanced drones has made my work

considerably easier to accomplish. The prototypes were a success. The project can now accelerate to levels never before imagined!

They have been programmed in detail to perform every conceivable task, to process extensive data at astonishing speeds. They are the perfect artificial people, one might say. To anyone unfamiliar with M-2's results at this point, it might sound like lunacy, but it is the truth.

On the unfortunate side, the efficiency of the drones also means it was no longer necessary to keep my assistants on the payroll. I was sorry to see them go, as they have definitely put in their share of work here, but it was a logical step forward. All great movements have a few casualties. Sometimes it is necessary in striving for the betterment of all.

Year Three, February, Day Twenty–Two

In these metallic halls, the drones are born. They work alongside me and exist for the cause they were created to fulfill. They are rather like me, without quite as many flaws.

They are not people. They are machines. It would seem unfathomable that machines could be considered as substitutes for real flesh-and-blood people, yet it only makes sense. This realization frightens me. It is disturbing that a machine can bypass a human in so many aspects and is not impaired by many of the qualities that define us as humans.

I will see this through to the end. It is far too late to turn back now. M-2 is a success, and has progressed beyond all of our expectations.

Why, then, am I having these misgivings?

Year Three, July, Day Six

My work at M-2 is done. I was dismissed today, and it was made clear to me that I will not be called back. They are replacing me with a drone, one superior to me in every way. Almost everything I know of the project is programmed into these artificial minds, so it appears there is no further need to keep me around.

My superiors were released months earlier, machines replacing them as well. Who is pulling the strings of the project now? I honestly do not know.

I know only that as a human, I am obsolete, outdated. There is no further need for me or my kind. M-2 ultimately desires progress built upon a foundation of order and control—not a mind.

Year Three, July, Day Seven

Since my removal from M-2, I have become fixated on the situation. I am beginning to believe that the focus of M-2 was lost to me. My fascination with it has shifted to a fearful obsession. What sort of future is due humanity if such a profound achievement as M-2 ever falls into the wrong hands?

Something dark lingers beneath the surface of M-2, I can sense it. The elusive network of data made available to me at M-2 now seems nothing more than a facade designed to lead me blindly through the motions of my once-esteemed services to the project. Before it is too late, I must have answers. I must have closure. My peace of mind depends on it.

It may still be possible for me to access the database if my passwords have not been changed. Tonight, I will make a secret entrance into the compound and do whatever I must to uncover the truth behind M-2.

Year Three, July, Day Eight

I have sat, pen in hand, staring at the page for hours, broken and uncertain. How should I end this? I have decided to merely relate the events as they occurred, for with its conclusion, there is nothing more.

I took my key card and my handgun and stole into the compound under the cover of darkness. I abhor violence, but I was concerned for my safety and felt the weapon to be a necessary evil in what I must do. The odds were that I would never have to use it, I reasoned.

My key card was still active and I had little difficulty entering the compound. I made my way back to my old office.

I sat at my computer terminal and used my passwords, which

had not yet been altered, to access the M-2 database. Areas of the database had always been kept confidential, even to one of my standing, but with time, I thought, I could infiltrate them.

Hours later, success rewarded my ceaseless patience. My suspicions had been correct. I found a detailed summary concerning M-2 in which the project's directive was linked to a greater agenda. Stunned, I read of incredible plans to replace key individuals of noteworthy status and influence with mechanized drones of identical physical appearance.

While scanning over the text, I heard footsteps approaching the office. A figure stepped into the room and flicked the light switch. I promptly found myself face-to-face with myself.

M-2 had replaced me with a drone in my likeness. At that second, I realized M-2 had replaced me in every sense of the word.

It stared at me, its synthetic features mirroring my own surprised expression. As it turned to leave, I knew it would sound the alarm and draw attention to my presence in the compound. I could not allow its escape.

I realized the pistol's report would draw unwanted attention, but I stood a better chance in firing than in letting the drone escape. I raised the pistol and fired into its back. It dropped.

I heard more footsteps and realized others were in my area of the compound. The shot had alerted them. I came to my feet and ran to make my exit. Because of my familiarity with the compound, I managed to elude much of the security as I slipped out.

Some of the security drones caught up with me as I jumped into my vehicle and screeched out of the neighboring parking lot. They fired shots in a bid to disable my car. A bullet tore through my left shoulder. Despite the pain, I continued to accelerate and managed to escape.

In the back of my mind, I regretted not copying the files needed to incriminate and expose M-2 for its role it what would undoubtedly become a grim future. My passwords would be changed and security would be tripled. I would never again have an opportunity.

I drove to a remote, secluded area on the outskirts of town, paranoid that if my identity had been confirmed during the earlier incident, authorities might be sent to my home to find me. I needed time to think. At least the wound in my shoulder was not serious enough to require immediate medical attention.

I looked down at the bullet wound then, and saw the exposed circuitry.

I sat, weakly holding my ballpoint pen, unable to fathom my place in the world and at a loss as to what to write in my journal.

Those at M-2 had decided not to replace a human with a machine, but to replace an older model with a newer, updated version. My release from M-2 was the rejection of an inferior drone, and my subsequent desire to defy M-2 nothing more than a malfunction.

Knowing what I am, I realize now that much of my life has been the product of an artificial memory chip. Everything I have known from my childhood until my first year at M-2 has been nothing more than an elaborate fabrication. My hopes and dreams are part of a programmed identity.

I have lived a lie. My manufactured life is nothing more than unwanted scrap without a purpose.

With nowhere else to turn and nothing else to say, I conclude this, my final entry.

Walls Between Worlds

His world was small and rectangular. The walls and the floor were drab and featureless. The ceiling was white. The room's only source of light came from a small box against one wall, with a screen that currently featured thousands, perhaps millions, of black and white dots scrambling in a maniacal dance. A cot stretched beside the opposite wall where he lay staring in vegetative silence at the monotonous, but captivating, screen.

He sat up on the edge of the cot, his bare feet coming to rest on the floor. After a pause, he stood and walked toward the other section of his tiny world, the bathroom.

The bathroom was barely large enough to accommodate a sink, a toilet, and a scum-layered bathtub. He picked up his toothbrush and the tube of paste which rested in the sink's basin, but stopped to look into the wall-mounted mirror.

Every day, he grew older. Minor changes crept over his features. He had grown taller.

He squeezed the gooey substance onto the bristles of the brush, his routine for as long as he could remember, and scrubbed his teeth. His mind drifted to one of the many curiosities of his world. Where did toothpaste come from?

As time wore on, he found his mind budding with more questions about everything around him. The box often initiated these inquisitive sparks when he gazed into its window to view those strange other places.

He rinsed his mouth out, rinsed the brush, and dropped it back into the sink, along with the tube of toothpaste. Looking down at the bathtub, he saw the small, worn white bar of soap lying near the drain. He decided not to take his bath just yet and walked out of the bathroom.

He approached the box and turned the dial until he could hear its sounds. The dots on the screen continued to race. He turned the other dial to change the screen's view. He turned it several times until the way was clear for him to look into the World of Wonder.

What an incredible world it was, filled with the treasures of his most imaginative dreams. He beheld pretty, sparkling things called diamonds, sapphires, and cubic zirconium. There were colorful things, stuffed animals. The box showed him interesting things, comic books and pocketknives. Then there were things he could not understand, such as compact discs, sewing kits, and a medley of assorted small machines.

Despite its bizarre nuances, the World of Wonder drew him in like nothing else could. It proved a fantastic escape from reality, his only reprieve from a life of monotony. He often sat on the edge of his bed and stared into the screen, mesmerized by its sights and sounds.

In the World of Wonder, there were others somewhat like him, but different—Jim, Bill, and Diane. Diane had long, lustrous golden hair. All three of them wore a baffling variety of clothing that changed with each viewing.

He had gotten used to this, but he could never grasp the full meaning. Was the World of Wonder a real place, or did it amount to fantasy, a trick of the special box?

Today, Diane showed a pretty collection of stuffed animals. She kept repeating the phrase, "twenty–nine, ninety–nine," but the meaning of the phrase was lost on him.

The sound of two surfaces sliding together caught his attention. At the small opening in the wall, he found his meal as expected, and the opening quickly slid shut.

The paper plate held a glob of boiled noodles, some mixed vegetables, and a piece of bread. He picked it up and stopped to listen. Sometimes the Voice spoke, sometimes it didn't. This time, silence met his ears. He returned to the bed and sat down to eat his meal. Minutes passed, becoming hours, and then his personal world shook at its foundation.

The walls between worlds were thinner than he had ever imagined.

Panic seized him. He toppled from his bed and into the floor with a cry, curling into a ball. He whispered to himself and hid his eyes.

A door between his world and another had sprung open. He saw others, people like him, like Bill, Jim, and Diane, and this time unconfined by the screen of the box. They had walked through the open door and into his world.

* * *

Charles Wilkinson rested against the hard, uncomfortable back of the kitchen chair. The living room sofa would have been kinder to his aging frame, but he didn't care today. Nothing really mattered to him now but the news he had received hours before—news that his only son, who had vanished all those years ago, had been located.

It stunned him at first, then elated him, but something still weighed on him.

For hours, Charles sat in front of a cold cup of coffee, his mind distant in thoughts of the detective's description of that place where Daniel had been and the man who had kidnapped him and kept him under lock and key.

The abductor, Andrew Brand, had kept Daniel enclosed in a prison, isolated unto himself but feasibly nourished. Brand had a history of mental illness. It was likely he would end up locked away in some institution, but until that time, he remained in custody, awaiting the decision on the matter of his crimes and instability.

Daniel had not been physically abused in any discernible way. The only apparent abuse had been a product of his isolation. Brand had spoken to Daniel on occasion through the locked door, but never made himself visible to the boy. He had slipped Daniel's meals through a small sliding panel, as well as soap, toothpaste, toilet paper, and other necessary items. Other than brief instances of verbal communication from Brand which Daniel may or may not have understood, the only stimulation Daniel had known during his captivity was the old television occupying the room. The television had been in disrepair and would only pick up one station, the CLG Shopping Network.

The phone rang again. Charles caught it on the first ring.

"Yes," he breathed into the phone. "I'll be there right away."

He tapped on the bedroom door. Marla, who had shut herself into the bedroom since the news came, answered. Words were unnecessary. She knew immediately, grabbed her purse, and they left. The time had come.

The drive seemed endless to Charles. The anticipation devoured him alive.

"Charles," Marla said, pointing. "The turn!"

Charles caught it just in time. He cut it sharply and whipped into the parking lot in front of the brick building. He and Marla exited the car and began their walk to the building. Charles slipped his hand around Marla's. As they walked, they looked ahead to the building and its large wooden doors. Behind those doors, they knew, their son waited for them.

"Mr. Wilkinson?" the officer spoke, breaking through Charles's jumbled thoughts. Charles didn't immediately answer, transfixed by the boy who stood to the officer's left.

It was Daniel, no question, but years older and pale from spending so many years locked indoors. His light-blond hair had been cut in a careless fashion. He had probably done the job himself. His eyes darted around with an intense mixture of awe and confusion.

"Mr. Wilkinson?" repeated the officer.

"Daniel!" Marla shouted hysterically. She bolted across the room to grab her son in both arms. "Oh, Daniel. You've finally come home." She held her son, sobbing, and he gawked at her, his eyes wide.

"Yes, sir, I'm Charles Wilkinson," Charles said to the officer. "Thank you so much. All of you." He looked around to the gathering of police officers and medical personnel. "I don't know how we can ever thank you enough for finding him and bringing him back into our lives."

"It's part of why we're here, Mr. Wilkinson," the officer replied. He paused, searching for a way to deliver his next words. "Your son doesn't know his own name. He isn't aware his name is Daniel Wilkinson. He doesn't respond to it. There are only a few words I've heard him say, but he's mentioned a stuffed koala and a panda. He said 'Sterling 200 Series pocketknife,' and he's named a couple of different comic books."

"The TV," Charles realized aloud. "That must be it. It would only pick up that shopping network, right?"

"Yes, and it's been drilled into his head for years, Mr. Wilkinson," the officer said. "I thought I should warn you ahead of time."

Charles nodded uncertainly. The officer parted a moment later. A specialist came forward to explain to Charles and Marla the details of the therapy, Daniel's hopeful steps to rehabilitation following the incident.

While Charles listened, he looked again to his wife and son. The path to recovery would not be an easy one, but their son was theirs again. He could only hope this was not another dream and he wouldn't wake up in the night without a son like all of those times before.

* * *

"I don't understand," Charles told Dr. Bauer, Daniel's therapist. "I mean, I understand he was traumatized, held prisoner by that sick—"

"Charles," Dr. Bauer interceded. He held up a hand. "What's important is that we do our best to work with him now. Daniel was there for many years and no one really knows how he's going to develop because of this, but we must believe the determining factor is in our own behavior. We can be hopeful, but we should also be careful."

"My son can't attend public school," Charles said heavily. "He can't even go out into public. All those years stolen from him and stolen from us as a family. I just..." Charles dropped his head and rubbed his eyes, which began to brim with tears.

Bauer sighed and placed a hand on Charles's shoulder. "The most important thing of all is that he's back, Charles. You and Marla have your son back. You can be a family again. It's going to take some work, that's all. We'll keep trying."

Charles dropped into the padded tan chair. He looked idly at the small table and the dish of candy on top of it—or cough drops, he couldn't tell for certain—while his mind worked to sort through his thoughts and fears.

"So far, these sessions have been useless," Charles said, his eyes fixed on the dish. "My son doesn't seem to understand or respond to much of anything. He'll watch television if we leave it on the CLG Shopping Network. The other channels seem to scare him."

"Charles, listen to me," Dr. Bauer said, and leaned forward as he spoke. "What's best for your son's well-being, and for your family, is for you and your wife to acclimate him to a normal life. He's with the ones who love him. They say time heals, Charles. In my experience, there's truth to that. We'll keep chipping away at his shell, and sooner or later, we're bound to break through."

* * *

Marla poured herself a rum and cola. She walked into the living room to fall into the folds of the sofa.

They had their long-lost son back and they could be a family again, couldn't they? Shouldn't she be happy?

Marla never recalled drinking as much as she had in the past few days. Maybe, she mused, the reality was too frightening to face sober.

Her own son, whom she had always loved so much even during his absence, had devolved into something alien. Charles, meanwhile, kept hoping and trying. As a wife and a mother, Marla knew she should share in the effort, but what could she do? And of everything her husband had done, what had made any difference?

She stood, the glass of dark rum-cola in her hand, and walked into the back bedroom. Her husband stood next to the bed, emptying the shopping bags onto it. This was Daniel's room, with blank walls and no decoration—only a bed, chest of drawers, and a television set.

"We really need to hang some pictures in here," Marla remarked in a quiet voice.

An assortment of gifts covered the bed. Since Daniel had become obsessed with many of the products sold on the CLG Shopping Network, Charles had made the gift purchases there, surprises for their son. *Welcome home, son.*

There were toys and games, including a hand-held electronic game, and comic books, some of the titles which Charles had heard his son mention. He had also included the Sterling 200

Series pocketknife, though he knew he would have to watch Daniel carefully with it and instruct him in its safe use, but he had made the purchase anyway because his son had taken such a liking to it from the sales pitches on television.

An abundance of stuffed animals also sat on the bed, including a fluffy red teddy bear, a large stuffed panda, and a smaller stuffed koala.

"He's going to love this," Marla murmured. Charles put an arm around her.

"I really hope so," he said. "I talked to Dr. Bauer about it. That's the main reason Daniel had a private session today—so we could have this ready for him when he got back."

"It was nice of Dr. Bauer to offer to drive Daniel home this time."

Charles nodded with a forced half-smile. "He's been very helpful through this. He should be dropping Daniel off in around ten minutes or so."

"I can't wait to see the look on our son's face." Marla finally managed a weak smile of her own. After another sip of her drink, she leaned against her husband. "You know, I haven't seen our son smile, not even once, since he's been home."

They walked to the living room together. The knock came within minutes. Charles answered the door. It was Dr. Bauer, there to drop Daniel off. Charles thanked the man.

Once Bauer was gone, Charles led his son down the hall to his room. Marla followed.

"Son, I've got a surprise for you," Charles said. He rested his hands on Daniel's shoulders and guided his son to the bedroom with Marla right behind.

Daniel halted inside the bedroom's doorway. He surveyed the numerous gifts on the bed's surface and his eyes stretched open wide. He looked from the hand-held video game to the comic books to the Sterling 200 Series pocketknife. His eyes grew larger. His stare settled on the stuffed animals.

A high-pitched noise came from him, faint at first, but growing in volume. It gave way to a terrible screeching sound. His eyes filled with tears. He screamed, confronted and overwhelmed by everything he had ever wanted, and his distinction of reality and fantasy cracked.

* * *

In a quiet room, Charles and Marla Wilkinson's eyes met for an instant. Both quickly resumed looking around the unfamiliar room. The walls needed repairing. When their eyes met again, the husband's gaze dropped.

"I know," Marla said, tragically reassuring. She laid a hand on top of his. "There's nothing else we could do. We aren't just telling ourselves that. That's why we fought them all to get here—even Bauer. They couldn't understand. I guess what I'm trying to say is—I never wanted to destroy our son, Charles, and I know you never did, either."

Charles and Marla shared a moment of silence. Across the house, newly purchased by the couple at a desperate sum, there was a door with an unusual, small sliding-panel opening. Behind it, a world away, their son shared the silence.

In a small, rectangular room within the house once owned by the incarcerated Andrew Brand, Daniel laid on the bed and watched the dark television screen for minutes on end until his eyes closed to the broken world. When he awoke, it would be whole again.

The Capellan Dream

The brush danced between a wild, sweeping assault and the precise, experienced brush strokes of a virtuoso. The dark oil colors were layered upon the canvas with intense deliberation until at moments the nameless muse within Nathan Capella urged him to fling the vivid images into being before they changed or even vanished altogether. He stopped to squint at the painting, then resumed lavishing the melancholy mixture of colors onto the canvas.

He leaned back to survey his work, setting the long-handled brush down between the palette and a small jar of linseed oil. He drank in the extraordinary quality of the accomplishment and a smile crossed his features. He had done it, at last, for the second time in his life.

Nathan had created many works of art in his lifetime, but two in particular were like nothing he had ever created: the one in front of him at this moment, and the first, which he had titled *Mountains in the Sky*.

With *Mountains in the Sky,* he had captured what he could only explain as something magical. When he awoke one morning to find the painting gone, he was completely stunned.

It had been before the divorce. He had helped out a friend, Ray, who had fallen on grueling times. Nathan's wife at the time, Aimee, had grudgingly allowed it.

Nathan regretted it the day Ray left without warning, making off with Nathan's prized work of art. Outraged, he had left to find Ray and address the situation, but he never learned where Ray had gone until months later at an art exhibition, when he found a large number of people praising Ray's monumental work of art which happened to be *Mountains in the Sky*.

Nathan attacked his former roommate in a fury. Those attending the exhibit had to drag him off of Ray. He was thrown out and arrested soon after. No one believed *Mountains in the Sky* had been his own creation. Even his friend Jay, who had tried to be sympathetic about the ordeal, had remained skeptical about Nathan Capella's claim.

Ray went on to acquire fame and prestige for the stolen work, although his own works met with disparaging criticism because he had never been a decent artist to begin with. Nathan failed in his attempts to recreate a piece of equal splendor to *Mountains in the Sky*. No matter what creative approach he tried, he could never revisit that segment of his soul that had spawned his first awe-inspiring work. It almost seemed as if the painting had painted itself, using his hands, and he could not force such a creative phenomenon knowingly through his own standard talent and ability. Through many subsequent unsuccessful attempts, Nathan trashed a sizable portion of his income on wasted canvas, paints, and supplies.

He seldom paid attention to his wife anymore, instead devoting his passion to the brush and canvas. He spent, or "wasted," their finances on chasing a childish dream, according to Aimee. When Aimee left him and filed for a divorce, he found himself struggling financially to keep his dreams afloat.

His present artistic endeavor had proven to be different from all of the others. Finally, he had surpassed even *Mountains in the Sky*. It was twistedly beautiful. There was something missing, though, some imperfection which he couldn't place despite staring at the painting until the phone's ring startled him.

He jolted in his seat and almost knocked over the linseed oil. He picked up the phone, preparing to hang up with the likelihood of this being another annoying telemarketer, when he heard a familiar voice on the other end.

"Hello?" the voice said. "Is this Nathan Capella?"

"Jay?" Nathan asked, surprised.

"Yeah, it's me," Jay replied. "How's it going? What have you been up to?"

"About the same," Nathan replied.

"Still searching for that perfect artistic expression?" Jay inquired in an amused tone.

"I believe I've found it," Nathan said to him. He looked to his painting and couldn't help feeling a bit smug.

"Really?" Jay responded, suddenly sounding rather disinterested. "Well, anyway, I was going to give you a call because I'm in town. I thought maybe Corinne and I would stop by and say hello, if that's all right with you?"

"Corinne?"

"My wife," Jay clarified. "You did hear I was married now, right?"

"Oh, of course."

"She's a blossoming artist like yourself," Jay said. "You might actually have something to talk about."

"Who knows?"

"But since I was in town, and it's been forever..."

"Sure, come on by, Jay. It *has* been a long time."

* * *

"Long time no see," Jay exclaimed, grabbing Nathan's hand and shaking it as he slapped his old friend on the shoulder. Jay was tall, well over six feet in height, and in good athletic shape. He stopped for a second to brush off the front of his brown sweater before proceeding in.

"And this is my wife, Corinne," Jay introduced.

Corinne was a lovely woman with long, wavy sienna-colored hair and dark-brown eyes. She held a small leather purse over one shoulder as she walked in after her husband.

Nathan treated them to a warm smile. He closed the door behind the couple, invited them to sit down, and offered them a drink before taking a seat himself.

"So how's life been treating you?" Jay asked as he sipped on the beer Nathan brought him. The two fell into conversation, reminiscing about old times, while Corinne looked around the room.

Cheap stock pictures and empty hooked hangers covered the walls. Nathan had displayed none of his own paintings anywhere in sight.

"So you said on the phone you've come up with something new?" Jay asked of Nathan, pulling Corinne's attention back into the conversation. "Like I said, Corinne's an up-and-coming artist herself."

"Oh?" Nathan said with a polite smile to Corinne. "What do you work with?"

"Oils, acrylics, pastel," she responded. "I have a lot of works I keep at home, but I didn't think to bring any with me, sorry. I would love to see some of yours, though—that is, if you don't mind."

"Well, actually, I only have one," Nathan admitted. "The latest."

"I would love to see that one," she said with a pleasant smile.

"It's still a work-in-progress," Nathan explained. "I haven't quite finished it yet, but it's almost done."

"You don't have to show it to me if you don't want to," Corinne said, "but I would be flattered if you brought it out. Jay tells me you're terrific at what you do."

"Come on, Nathan," Jay chided. "We'll only be in town another day. Let's see what you've got. The way you were talking about it over the phone, well hell, I've never heard you that excited."

"Okay," Nathan caved, getting up. "Come on."

He beckoned them after him as he went into the back room where he kept all of his art supplies. They followed him into the small room where the easel stood upright, bearing his latest painting.

"I give to you *Angelique*—the Capellan Dream." Jay and Corinne gazed at the painting in silence.

The girl in the painting was small, no older than seven, with an unusual glimmer of green in her eyes and short, brown hair that fell shy of being shoulder-length. She wore a small, pink blouse and a matching skirt. She looked out from the painting with an expression that was almost bashful. A crisscross pattern of gold-on-maroon comprised the background.

Something in the young girl's eyes appeared off-center. The girl's posture was somehow strange as well. In some way, she was tainted beneath the surface.

But something was missing. As Nathan Capella had mentioned, the painting was unfinished.

"Sweetie?" Jay said, gently shaking his wife. Corinne looked to her husband, startled as Jay's voice broke through her fascination.

"It's wonderful," she said, a bit breathless, as she looked over to Nathan. "You're really a talented artist, more talented than I could ever hope to be. Everything I have ever done pales in comparison to this."

"Thank you," Nathan said to her, receiving the praise with grace. "Like I said, it's still a work-in-progress. Once I finish it, I'll be ready to unveil it to the public."

"You are one-of-a-kind," Corinne said to him, her eyes full of honest veneration, "and I can honestly say I connect with this—with Angelique. I think a lot of other people will, too."

Jay regarded his wife with a strange glance. "Sweetie, maybe we should go," he said. He turned to give Nathan a quick, firm handshake. "Good seeing you again. I'll give you a shout before we leave town, okay? Take care." He pulled his wife along as he moved for the door. Nathan saw them out, a bit confused by the couple's odd behavior as they walked to the sleek gray luxury sedan outside and drove away.

* * *

The following day, Nathan sat in front of *Angelique,* staring at the young girl with the short, brown hair and green eyes.

The knock at his front door surprised him. He stood to answer it. Jay and Corinne waited outside.

"Just stopping by one last time before we head out of town," Jay said. "Everything all right?"

"Sure," Nathan answered. "Come on in."

"So," Jay said, breaking the quiet with a change of tone once the three relaxed, "when do you think you'll be finished with your new painting?"

"I'm not sure yet," Nathan replied. Jay and Corinne looked at one another, their expressions vague.

"Okay," Jay said. He shifted in his seat on the couch, "I have an offer for you. We'd like to buy it. I realize it isn't finished, but—"

"It isn't for sale."

"I'll pay anything," Corinne blurted.

Nathan looked at her. It struck him now that it was Corinne who desired his newest work, to such an extent that she had come here to make an offer.

"I wish I could help," Nathan said to her, "but this is something special to me. I can't sell it. I would love for you to be there at its first showing, though." He stood, feeling uncomfortable and looking for a way to break the mounting tension. He turned toward the kitchen. "Do either of you want a drink?"

"I'll go with a beer, if you've got one," Jay called. Nathan nodded and walked into the kitchen. He heard the soft footsteps behind him a second too late. Something crashed into the back of his head, and as he collapsed face-first into the floor, darkness took him.

* * *

Someone shook him and slapped him on the cheek a couple of times. Nathan opened his eyes.

He sprawled on his back on the hard linoleum kitchen floor. Corinne crouched beside him. Jay stood across the room, looking away. Nearby, the painting, *Angelique,* rested against the refrigerator.

Nathan tried to sit up, but found it impossible. Wire bound his arms and ankles. When he struggled against it, it cut into his flesh with biting unpleasantness.

"What's happening?" Nathan muttered, groggy and trying to piece it all together.

"We didn't want to do it this way," Corinne explained, "but I don't think you understand the caliber of what you've created. One way or another, I came here today knowing I would leave with this painting."

"That's why you two knocked me out and tied me up?" Nathan said, his voice rising with incredulity. "You came here to steal my art?"

"After seeing *Angelique,* Jay told me he now believes what you told him about being the creator of *Mountains in the Sky.* Who else could it have been but you? I can't begin to describe what I felt after I looked at her, at Angelique. I realized she was meant for me. Speaking as an artist, do you realize what something like this could do for my reputation? This could launch the career I've always dreamed of. *Mountains in the Sky* was powerful and successful, and this is leagues beyond that."

"It isn't even finished!" Nathan exclaimed, his anger heating to a monstrous burning rage. They couldn't do this! For the second time in his life, his greatest work was being seized from him!

"And that's why I need you," Corinne said with a devious smile. "I want to know what's missing from the painting."

"To hell with you!" Nathan shouted. "Jay, you can't let her do this! " Jay turned slightly, but he wouldn't meet Nathan's gaze.

"What is missing from the painting?" Corinne repeated.

"I don't know," Nathan spat at her. "And if I did, I would never tell you." As he spoke, Corinne stood and walked around him, out of his line of sight. Jay walked out of the room.

"That's okay," he heard Corinne say. "I'll do it with or without you."

"You aren't even a real artist," Nathan continued with spite, "to take credit for work you stole from someone else. In my eyes, there's nothing lower and more pitiful, aside from someone who stabs his own friend in the back for profit." When he said this final piece, he raised his voice to ensure Jay would hear him. "And if relying on my ability is the only way you can ever hope to achieve—"

He stopped, realizing that someone was close behind him, propping him up since he couldn't sit up on his own. A cold metal wire much like the wire around his wrists and ankles encircled his throat and jerked taut. The wire tightened, constricting and cutting off any further attempts to draw air.

"Nothing personal," Corinne whispered as she strangled him with quiet, vicious determination, "but I can't have you around trying to take credit for your own work, now can I?"

He tried to pull away, but couldn't. He wilted from lack of oxygen. The wire bit into his flesh, burning.

"If it's any consolation," Corinne continued, "you've made me one very happy girl." She wrapped the wire around each of her hands once more to stabilize her grip, and planting her knees against his back for leverage, she yanked the wire with all of her strength and a cruel twist. The cold wire sliced through the skin of Nathan's throat and blood spurted freely from his neck.

Corinne's heart skipped a beat when his blood sprayed onto the painting. Tears of crushed passion came to her eyes at the blood-stained canvas, surely ruined, but her tears halted with the epiphany of the girl in the painting. Nathan saw it as well, even as he died in Corinne's choking grip, fading forever and never to be known for the works he had created.

As Nathan's body went soft and lifeless, Angelique stared back at Corinne through a haze of blood. Corinne understood at last what had been missing from the painting.

Angelique, the Capellan Dream, was now complete.

Metal Scars

I: 2:00 a.m. in the City of Industry

Angela Holt walked into the building, little more than an over-
sized storage shed, and threw a quick nod to the three men who
accompanied her. Two of them slid the front doors closed. The
other one switched on a battery-powered lantern. Its pale light
cast a dull glint against the spare mechanical parts and scrap
metal stored here.

The group had arrived early. Angie would have it no other
way. She considered herself allergic to failure. Some called it
paranoia. Angie didn't care. To her, it was an advantage in this
line of work. You didn't leave room for mistakes when your father was Jeremiah Holt, a man feared and respected by many in
the criminal underworld.

Most knew by now that Angie lacked the patience of her father. Being her father's daughter was a sting of insecurity most
could only recognize as a vicious temper. Partially due to this,
the men who accompanied her knew to keep their mouths shut
and their fingers on the triggers.

From streets away, a man approached the location of the
meeting point. He carried a brown paper sack, folded at the top,
in one hand. His other hand reached into his pocket and produced a handful of assorted pieces: springs, bits of wire, and
metal shavings. He popped them into his mouth, swallowed them
down, and proceeded around the bend toward his destination.

This man, otherwise ordinary in appearance, had known
many names but was most widely known, for obvious reasons, as
the Man Who Eats Metal.

He paused in front of the double doors. He gave two taps, as
agreed upon, and turned the handle on one of the side-by-side
doors to slide it open.

Inside, Angie's face was white in the light of the lantern.
"Close the door," she said.

The Man Who Eats Metal stepped in and slid the door shut
without comment. He turned around with one arm outstretched,
the one holding the paper sack. One of the men came forward to

take the sack, looked inside, counted the bundle of bills within, and nodded to Angie.

"It's all here," he said.

If the Man Who Eats Metal held any awareness of the men who stood in the darkness with deadly gun barrels trained on him, he gave no indication. Angie continued to stare at the man and called, without looking back, "Stanton. Bring it out."

A figure at the back end of the shed brought a black duffel bag forward and tossed it onto the floor. The Man Who Eats Metal blinked and walked to it. He crouched to open the duffel bag. Multiple smaller bags of snow-white filled it.

The Man Who Eats Metal glanced up. He motioned to one of the bags. It took a moment for Angie to understand what the gesture meant. She nodded.

"Be my guest. Stanton, give him a taste."

Stanton pulled out a switchblade and flicked the blade out. He approached to slip the tip of the blade into one of the bags, only a slight break, and held up the flat of the blade with a tiny mound of white atop its end. The Man Who Eats Metal leaned forward, pressed one nostril shut, and snorted the white candy through the other. Eyes closed, he leaned his head back.

A moment later, the Man Who Eats Metal's eyes opened. A smile spread across his lips. He approved.

"Then we have a deal, I assume," Angie said, her eyes steel. Stanton sealed the duffel bag, lifted it from the floor, and passed it to the Man Who Eats Metal, who accepted it and stood, bundling the bag to his chest.

The Man Who Eats Metal shuffled a few steps to the metal doors. He adjusted the bag to free one arm and placed his hand on the door's cold handle. Angie's eyes bored into his back, calculating, working at some uncompleted equation in the folds of her mind.

"Wait," Angie said. The Man Who Eats Metal paused, having slid the door only halfway open.

"Where have I seen you before?" Angie asked.

The Man Who Eats Metal answered with a shrug. Angie continued to stare. Her mind worked to piece together the escaped memory, but it proved fruitless. She pulled the pistol from her waistband, looked to Stanton, and gestured at the Man Who Eats Metal, who still faced away from her.

"Check him."

The Man Who Eats Metal turned around. Stanton came toward him with his handgun drawn. "Put down the bag," Stanton ordered.

The Man Who Eats Metal set the duffel bag down. He looked at Stanton with the hint of a raised eyebrow, and then looked at Angie, but said nothing. Stanton patted him down and took a step back. "Raise your shirt."

The Man Who Eats Metal hesitated, so Angie stepped in. "Do what he says," she said. The other men in the back of the shed took careful aim on the Man Who Eats Metal. He appeared bewildered, but complied with their demands. The gray shirt came up. Stanton peered at his chest.

"He's not wearing a wire," Stanton said. "Not that I can see."

"But what is *that?*" Angie said, focusing through the dim lighting on the Man Who Eats Metal's exposed torso. She and Stanton looked to the Man Who Eats Metal, expecting an answer, and neither could resist a prolonged stare at the nasty vertical scar that ran from the man's navel to the middle of his chest.

The Man Who Eats Metal did not answer. He lowered his shirt with a bit of caution and adjusted it at the ends while the others still watched him.

Angie studied the Man Who Eats Metal's eyes for a lengthy duration and finally answered, "We're done here." She flipped a wave of dismissal, but continued to watch the Man Who Eats Metal as he hefted the drug-filled duffel bag, opened the sliding metal door the rest of the way, and exited.

What was it, a surgery scar? An incision right down the front of the sternum? No. To Angie, something wasn't right about this.

After the man had gone, Angie looked to Stanton. "Follow him. Watch him." Angie glanced back to the rifle-bearing men, who looked to her expectantly. "Go with him."

If Stanton attributed Angie's decision to her sometimes unnecessary level of paranoia, he said nothing of it. He opened the doors as quietly as he could. The two others accompanied him outside to stalk the Man Who Eats Metal through the dark streets of the City of Industry.

Alone in the storage building, Angie opened the Velcro pack at her side and pulled out a radio. She leaned against the scrap metal bin, switched the radio on, and waited for Stanton's report. Minutes passed. When the static broke and Stanton's voice came through, it was quiet.

"Madison."

Angie responded. "Yes, De Soto?"

Stanton's voice replied in a hushed murmur. Angie held the radio closer to her ear.

"...something strange," Stanton was saying.

"What is it?" Angie asked.

A block away, Stanton and his two accomplice gunmen stood concealed behind the edge of a brick building. The Man Who Eats Metal had stopped on the side of the street with the duffel bag under one arm, reached into his pocket, and began eating—something. What startled Stanton was the glint of moonlight from the substance in the Man Who Eats Metal's hand.

Angie repeated her question over the radio. Stanton turned the sound down and continued to watch the Man Who Eats Metal. A bit of the metallic substance fell from the Man Who Eats Metal's hand. Once finished, he again took the duffel bag in both arms and proceeded along the street.

When the distance was safe enough to keep them unseen, Stanton moved ahead. He searched the ground for the fallen material, found it, and pulled into the shadows to respond to Angie.

"De Soto," spoke Angie's voice from the radio, impatience spiking her tone.

"Metal," Stanton whispered back. "He's eating metal. Little pieces of metal!"

"What? Are you sure?"

"Yes." Stanton glanced down the street, toward where the Man Who Eats Metal had walked in the opposite direction. "I'm dead sure."

When no immediate answer came, Stanton held up the radio to speak again, to make certain Angie had heard him, when Angie spoke.

"Lock and Load."

When Stanton hesitated, Angie's voice again broke the static.

"Are you listening, De Soto?"

Stanton held the radio closer. "Yes," he replied into it. He looked over to the others. "You heard her. Let's go."

"Don't delay," Angie added.

Stanton paused. Was it his imagination or did Angie's voice quiver a tiny bit?

Stanton gripped his pistol and the others raised their weapons accordingly. They moved in quick pursuit of the Man Who Eats Metal, closing in to take aim.

Back in the storage building, Angie leaned against the scrap bin for support.

"The Man Who Eats Metal," she whispered, realization sinking into her. Her cold visage concealed a splinter of dread. She gripped her pistol and watched the doors.

Minutes crawled by with no word from Stanton. Angie lifted the radio.

"De Soto." Silence.

"De Soto!"

Angie put the radio away, took a breath, and moved for the doors. She slid one of them open, just enough to make room for her exit, and walked out. With her gun at the ready, Angie prepared to fire at anything that moved as she strode along the streets of the City of Industry toward the still block that awaited.

II: The House of Eisler

Well across the countryside in his Louisiana home, Jeremiah Holt sat in bed, reading by lamplight. The shrill ring of the old-fashioned black telephone on his nightstand startled him.

He grunted and flopped his book face-down onto the bed beside him. He tossed his reading glasses aside and picked up the phone.

"Who's this?" he asked with a glance at his watch, a silver Rolex.

Jeremiah heard a shuddering breath before the voice spoke. "Something terrible has happened."

"Angela? Is that you?" Jeremiah hadn't heard his only daughter's voice in years, but if it was her, he noticed an uncharacteristic quality in her voice, an element he had never heard in it since her days of early youth—fear.

"I need to know something, Jeremiah," she asked.

Since her adolescence, even before she had become embittered against her father, Angie had referred to him by his first name. This call lacked the bite typical in Angie's tone on the rare occasions when she did speak to him, which piqued his curiosity all the more.

When Jeremiah didn't immediately speak, Angie continued. "You told me years ago about a man you met, a man who ate metal."

The phrase ignited a flare in Jeremiah Holt's mind, illuminating the catacombs of his memory. *The Man Who Eats Metal.* Yes, Jeremiah Holt remembered.

He had actually met the man twice, both times at Eisler's place many years ago. At the time, the man had been called— Ives, Jeremiah thought, though he couldn't recall exactly, but that sounded right. At first, the man had fallen into the background, overshadowed by Mr. Eisler himself.

Eisler was a well-dressed man with a neatly trimmed mustache and a voice bold and clear, a contrast to the freaks who populated the rest of his mansion. Jeremiah's impression was that he had just wandered into some deranged costume ball. Strains of Wagner's *Tristan und Isolde* distracted him, playing from the record that spun in a corner. Someone wearing a yellow sheet hovered near it.

A dirty girl with stringy, dripping hair popped up beside Jeremiah. Startled, and with no desire of ruining his suit, Jeremiah quickly stepped away.

Eisler laughed. The girl, covered from top to bottom in the brown oil, smiled. Even her teeth were oily, to Jeremiah's disgust.

"Cindy!" Eisler said. "Give our guest Mr. Holt some space, please!" He elbowed her aside and beckoned for Jeremiah Holt and Kenji Nakamura, also present, to follow. Eisler led them on the grand tour through his mansion, firing mass introductions about as they walked.

Jeremiah didn't care. He was there for business reasons, and so was Nakamura. Both men were concerned with Eisler's obscenely potent and abundant supply of white candy.

While Eisler boomed introductions and conversation, Jeremiah Holt met him for the first time, Ives, the Man Who Eats Metal. "Ives" was a man regular in appearance who might have slipped from his mind right away, but a small motion from his direction caught Jeremiah's eye.

He looked to the man and saw what was clearly the act of holding a handful of metal shavings up to the light and slipping them into his mouth. Jeremiah watched, fascinated, as the man swallowed them down. Though he found the act bizarre, he quickly learned that in the midst of Eisler's carnival of friends and fiends, anything might happen.

That was the day Jeremiah Holt and Kenji Nakamura began to do business with Eisler. It was the second meeting, the last day they ever visited the mansion, that would engrain the man into Jeremiah Holt's mind, as well as Nakamura's.

The situation changed with Eisler's abrupt lapse of communication. Repeated efforts to contact Eisler returned a maddening lack of success and eventually brought them to the front door of Eisler's home, armed and unannounced.

One of Nakamura's men had a long, narrow item wrapped in a white cloth secured on his back. Jeremiah had armed himself with his bulky .44 magnum, which he kept tucked beneath his jacket. The rest of the men were equipped with firearms and stood back in the dark of night, out of sight.

White ribbons fluttered from the two columns of the Eisler's front portico. Jeremiah stepped up to the door and, with the door's large brass bring, gave four heavy knocks.

When no answer met his attempt, he knocked again. They waited another half-minute before Jeremiah motioned to his men, who came forward.

At this point, the door opened slightly. A pale face, the top of its head bald and smooth, peeked out.

"We're here to see Eisler," Jeremiah said to it.

"My," the face said, surveying the lot beneath the portico.

"Eisler," Jeremiah repeated.

"Mr. Eisler is unavailable," the face replied.

"We are important associates of Mr. Eisler," Jeremiah Holt said, "and this is very important business."

"I am sorry."

Jeremiah glanced back. The stern-faced Nakamura returned his glance impassively. Jeremiah turned back to the bald figure and reached into his jacket to touch his .44 magnum. "If Eisler doesn't come out here to speak to us," he said, "we're coming in to see him."

The bald face withdrew. The door closed. Jeremiah heard the sound of the bolt sliding into place.

"He is going to tell Eisler?" Nakamura asked. Jeremiah only shook his head.

They waited outside. After some time, Jeremiah looked at his Rolex with dwindling patience. Nakamura's expression remained stony.

"Enough," Nakamura said. He directed his men toward the door. "Break it down."

Jeremiah moved clear. The two men in Nakamura's employ crashed against the door once, twice, shot the lock, kicked the door, and broke it wide open to pour in with guns drawn. Nakamura stepped in, followed by Jeremiah Holt with his .44 magnum out and the others right behind him.

The room appeared frozen still. The white figure who had first met them stared toward them from a corner, appearing whiter still, while multiple other figures stared at the group. Before Jeremiah could give any of it proper consideration, a large man wearing a tool belt and a motorcycle helmet and brandishing a pipe wrench rushed at them from one side.

Gunfire erupted. Bullets ripped through his body. He struck the floor. The pipe wrench skidded to a stop beside Jeremiah Holt's shoes.

Another fury-eyed individual, a man with a bull-ring in his nose and a long, sharp knife in each hand, charged across the room from behind the fallen man. With a cry of pain, one of Nakamura's men took a knife between the ribs. The rest opened fire and dropped the assailant. Two of the men rushed to attend to their fallen comrade, but another sudden motion caused them to whirl and fire again. Oily Cindy struck the floor, dead.

"We will kill as many of you as we must!" Nakamura declared to the room.

Despite the threat, some of those in the room, those nearest exits, fled from sight. Jeremiah still held his .44 magnum, and though he had not fired it yet, he remained vigilant.

Music played from the record player in the corner of the room. Jeremiah walked over and blasted a hole through it.

While Nakamura moved to assist the critically injured man among their number, Jeremiah scanned the room and spotted one he thought he recognized sitting on a stool to one side of the room. As uninteresting as he first appeared compared to the rest of his company, it was this quality that caused him to stand apart to Jeremiah. When he swallowed down the handful of metal bits in plain sight, Jeremiah's memory sparked.

"You," Jeremiah called to the man—Ives, he thought.

The man did not respond. Jeremiah walked over to confront him.

The man still looked around the room, at almost everything but Jeremiah himself. When he did look Jeremiah's way, he flinched at the long barrel of the .44 magnum pointed at his face.

"Your name is Ives, isn't it?" Jeremiah asked. The man appeared confused.

"Stop acting like a fool," Jeremiah said. "Don't waste my time. Where is Eisler?"

The man shook his head and shrugged.

"Enough of this," Nakamura said. He approached. Jeremiah decided to step away, but he watched.

Kenji Nakamura extended an open hand toward one of his men, who removed a cloth-wrapped item from its strapped position on his back. He unfolded it to reveal an exquisite shining blade, a sword of graceful curve and balance, which he placed in Nakamura's hand.

Nakamura's hand closed around the sword's hilt. He stepped toward Ives to level the gleaming metal at his chest.

"We will search this house until we find Eisler," Nakamura said. "You have nothing to gain by keeping secrets from us. All of you." Nakamura looked around the room, at all present who accompanied Ives. "You will do what I say and bring Eisler to us, or this man will die. Do you understand? I will give you five seconds." Nakamura looked back to Ives, sword primed. "Five."

No one else spoke. Jeremiah remained alert, his hand on his gun.

"Four," Nakamura said.

Nakamura's stare penetrated the man. Ives looked down.

"Three," Nakamura said.

The lines around Nakamura's eyes darkened.

"Two."

A pair of footsteps sounded. Men raised their guns. Whatever the intention might have been, the steps halted there.

"One."

Nakamura stared at Ives, the Man Who Eats Metal, whatever his actual name might be. Ives kept his eyes to the floor. When the last second expired, the man looked up to meet Nakamura's stare.

Nakamura's expression tightened in rage. *Zero.*

Nakamura struck. The blade sliced through shirt and flesh and rendered the Man Who Eats Metal open from chest to belly. The rest became lost to pandemonium.

Nakamura reeled. Jeremiah Holt squeezed the trigger of his .44 magnum, firing one explosive round and turning to flee with the others.

As for Nakamura, his work was done. The encounter left him blinded for life and permanently disfigured.

For a time afterward, police swarmed the place. They found Eisler's body behind the locked door of one of the home's top-floor bedrooms. His nostrils and mustache were powdered white. He had smashed every figurine and breakable item on his shelves, along with the mirrors, into pieces with a ball-peen hammer.

Jeremiah later found a set of photographs captured by one of his men before the business had gone sour, and he tacked one of these to the corkboard in the foyer of his home. He circled the man's image and wrote at the bottom of the photo, *Ives.* Soon after, he crossed it out. That wasn't really the man's name, after all, was it? Jeremiah wrote instead, *The Man Who Eats Metal.*

Little Angela had looked at the photo many times. By the time Jeremiah told his daughter the story behind it, she had entered early adolescence and questioned the story's authenticity.

Now, everything had changed. Today, she believed that, just after 2:00 a.m. in the City of Industry, she might have encountered the Man Who Eats Metal.

"Leave him alone," Jeremiah said into the phone's receiver. "If you have any sense at all, girl, you'll get as far away from him as you can!"

III: Lock and Load

The rhythmic throbbing of machinery was faintly audible on the block where Stanton and the gunmen stood against the wall of one building. Stanton motioned and slipped around the corner. The gunmen followed him with weapons readied.

They crept through the darker portion of the street in pursuit of the Man Who Eats Metal, who moved some distance ahead and around another corner. So far, he appeared oblivious to their approach.

When Angie ordered the man's death, her tone gave Stanton concern. He hoped not to underestimate his opponent, even when the opponent seemed harmless. Even a small, frightened rodent, when backed into a corner, could bite.

Then again, that strange note in Angie's voice might have been urgency. If time was of the essence, they would just sweep in and gun the man down without warning. Afterward, they would get out of here as quickly as possible. Yes, Stanton decided, that was the best way to do it.

The man's silhouette slipped to the left, around the corner of the building at the intersection ahead. Stanton quickened his pace. The gunmen exchanged glances. They moved in for the hit.

They came around the corner, fingers on triggers. To their momentary surprise, the Man Who Eats Metal stood there facing them with the duffel bag in his arms. A street lamp shone down on him like a spotlight.

The three men raised their guns to the Man Who Eats Metal. Without a word, they squeezed the triggers. Three thuds, muted by silencers, struck the unarmed man and the duffel bag hit the ground.

Pain corkscrewed through Stanton's mind, a world of pain he had never known or even imagined.

He staggered. His face, chest, stomach, and groin erupted as if wrung through a white-hot grinder. His threshold collapsed. He struck the pavement, writhing and gurgling, his nerves submerged in a river of fire and his thoughts scattered and trickling through the cracks of his suffering-scorched mindscape.

The deaths of the other two gunmen were instantaneous, their bodies forced to accommodate the metal-storm that issued from three bullet-holes, innumerable metallic fibers penetrating their skin, muscle, sinew, and organ tissue. They became lifeless, shredded bags of metal-embedded flesh on the sidewalk.

"De Soto," came Angie Holt's whisper from Stanton's radio, damaged and lying on the ground a distance along the street.

"De Soto!"

Minutes later, Angie crept onto the scene with her pistol in one hand. When she saw Stanton and presumably the accompanying gunmen, who were no longer recognizable, she gasped and backed away.

Besides Angie's own heavy breathing, only Stanton's gurgling rasps and faint splashing punctuated the silence. He floundered in his own blood and urine. His clothing and the front portion of his body were destroyed. The greater portion of his face had been sheared away. An eye protruded, gaping upward and outward. Countless metallic particles had infiltrated his exposed jawbone and glinted beneath the street light.

Angela Holt's pride fell to pieces. Before she ran, before she called Jeremiah and received the warning which came too late, she uncovered a deeply buried measure of compassion within herself. Standing over Stanton's flopping body, she put a bullet into the man's head and gave him peace.

Somewhere on the streets of the City of Industry, a man awoke on the floor of an abandoned warehouse. He felt weak and sluggish, his mind fogged as it often was on these occasions. With the remainder of a long-lost tongue, he tasted blood and metal. After spitting a mouthful of blood onto the floor, he discovered the duffel bag lying nearby and recognized its contents.

He spilled out a line of white and drew it in through one nostril. A hard wave of satisfaction struck him. He sighed, collapsing against a crate.

Yes, he thought. *That's what I like.*

His eyes flicked open. He dug a hand into one pocket and pulled out a handful of scrap yard trail mix.

Well, besides this. He swallowed the metal down.

Agony of Being

The clerk stared into the ominous black barrel of the gun, his eyes wide with shock. The pistol's hammer drew back with a click.

At the back of the store, the door to the men's restroom opened. Jack Redmond, in his gray suit and wire-rimmed glasses, stepped out. He walked toward the front counter, intent on buying a bottle of aspirin to relieve the headache that had persisted for the last half-hour, when he noticed the convenience store's only other customer held a gun.

The clerk's gaze diverted toward Jack. The armed man noticed, tensed, and whirled around. Fear stabbed into Jack's senses. He grabbed the man's wrist and wrenched it upward. A blast erupted from the gun's barrel, just missing the top of Jack's head.

The store clerk watched, open-mouthed and afraid, as the two men tumbled to the floor in a fight for the deadly pistol. An inner voice of reason pulled the clerk from his paralyzing fear. He turned and snatched up the phone to call the police.

The gun went off again. The clerk froze. His fingers gripped the phone tightly.

The robber leaped to his feet and ran for the store's glass front door. The clerk dashed around to the front of the counter. He gasped at the sight in front of him.

"Sir?" spoke the dispatcher's voice from the phone.

"Help," the clerk breathed. "We need help, *now!* Someone's been shot!"

Jack's glasses rested on the floor beside him, coated with blood. Blood covered the side of his face and formed a growing dark-red pool beneath his head.

* * *

Through an ocean of darkness...

A light broke through the stillness. Painful and bright, it

penetrated Jack's vision and roused him from his peace. His eyes fluttered open. He found himself lying between the thin, cool sheets of an immaculate white hospital bed. Everything was blurred. He realized he wasn't wearing his glasses.

"Mr. Redmond?" came the voice of an unrecognizable figure from nearby. "Can you hear me?"

"I'm not deaf, and I'm not stupid, either," Jack muttered, and tried to sit up.

"You're lucky to be alive," the voice answered concisely.

"I need to get out of here," Jack replied under his breath.

"You aren't going anywhere." Another of the room's blurry occupants walked over to Jack's bed and reached toward his face. Jack grabbed one of the hands and pushed it aside.

"Leave me alone," he mumbled.

"Mr. Redmond, these are your glasses," a female voice said, exasperated. Jack sighed and accepted the glasses from her. When he slid them onto his face, the room swam into focus.

Jack now clearly saw the nurse who had replaced his glasses as well as the white-coated doctor who had spoken. The doctor studied Jack from nearby, his hand resting on the end of the stethoscope around his neck.

"You'll have to remain until you've fully recovered," the doctor said, "and we'll have to keep you for further observation. You took a bullet to the head, Mr. Redmond. By all accounts, you should be thankful you're still here, and you aren't the only one. Your wife has been here constantly since your arrival. She's right outside.

"You have sustained a small amount of damage to the brain. We haven't been able to tell that any of the vital areas were harmed, but we have to be sure. We're going to keep you under close observation until your release. I know this news might be unsettling—but as before, you're a very lucky man."

Jack could only trust the doctor's word, but he digested the information with a mixture of abandon and denial. He reached up to feel the bandage around his head.

The doctor left the room. The nurse remained for a moment longer to take care of anything Jack might need, but he had no requests. She left a plastic cup filled with water on the small table beside his bed. He ignored it. Once the nurse left, his wife sprang into the room.

"Oh, honey," she choked out, her eyes full of tears. She ran forward and put her arms around him, kissing the top of his head.

Julia was as beautiful as ever, her thick, straight hair showering down in a rich, dark-brown abundance. Her deep, dark eyes were resilient with a sophistication he had always found attractive.

Jack relayed the doctor's news to his wife. Julia nodded. The doctor had already told her the same. She wanted to believe Dr. West's assurances, but she needed to see it with her own eyes. Jack's return to consciousness now filled her with the concrete, tactile hope she so terribly needed.

"I just need to rest," he told her almost an hour later. Her eyes were somber. Though reluctant, she understood.

"I'll get some lunch and come back a bit later," she said. "Do you want me to bring you anything?"

Jack shook his head. She kissed him and left.

Jack lay in bed, alone, and stared at the ceiling until he grew drowsy. He should have asked Julia to bring him some reading material at least, he thought, but it wasn't long before he drifted into sleep.

Mocking laughter resonated. Jack's body slammed viciously down. His face pressed against a cold, flat barrier. His jaundiced face was drawn tight and barely held together, like a jigsaw puzzle on the brink of falling apart. His eyes were devoid of anything but surrender.

Jack Redmond? That wasn't his name. He didn't know his true name, but his tormentor knew it and knew with a certain sadistic glee that it meant nothing.

Jack was helpless, his body weak and useless as his master exacted brutal whims upon him without end.

His eyes opened. He shook uncontrollably. He couldn't stop the tears. The fear, injustice, and horror of what he had seen overcame him.

"Mr. Redmond?" the nurse spoke, concern in her voice. Jack turned away to bury his face in the pillow, already damp from his tears, and continued to cry.

"Mr. Redmond, what's wrong?" the nurse pressed. She laid a hand on his shoulder.

Jack lifted his face from the pillow. What had he seen? What had he experienced?

"Do you need me to get Dr. West?" the nurse asked.

"I'll be all right," Jack managed to say to her. He wiped his eyes.

"Are you sure? You seem upset."

"It's okay," Jack said. He took a deep breath. "I—I think I just had a bad dream."

"If you need anything at all, let me know." The nurse left him. Jack remained in silence, unable to divert his thoughts from the torment he had known moments ago.

He was still trembling.

He knew he wouldn't be able to sleep now. He took the remote control from the bedside stand and turned on the room's single wall-mounted television.

* * *

Dr. West scanned the medical chart. "I see that Mr. Redmond's behavior has become increasingly erratic," he commented.

"He still refuses to sleep on his own," the nurse answered, "but the sedatives are helping. Still, he seems disturbed."

"It seems to be worsening," Dr. West remarked. "And these things he keeps saying—this bears a strange resemblance to the case we had with Mr. Brennan."

"I didn't know Mr. Brennan."

"Of course," Dr. West realized. "I don't believe you were with us back then. To the matter at hand, I suspect a psychological evaluation may be in order for Mr. Redmond. These nightmares are most likely a result of his trauma."

"Mr. Redmond believes these are more than nightmares," the nurse told him in a slightly puzzled voice, "and refuses to believe otherwise. To him, these things he's seeing—they're real."

* * *

Jack Redmond awoke in a cold sweat, unable to escape his torturous visions. Something bleak and hopeless had awakened within him, something submerged far beneath the surface of this mundane life. It did not, and could not, figure into his life of thirty-four years. It was beyond this life, the Before and the After. He remembered it, and he was certain it remembered him.

Recalling what had happened in the convenience store, he realized the robber who had almost killed him had been one of its vessels, a messenger.

This was but the first attempt of his unspeakable persecutor. Jack knew he could no longer remain here, under this constant barrage of sedatives, where he would remain vulnerable. He threw the sheets aside and climbed out of bed. As he stood, the nurse entered.

"Mr. Redmond, you need your rest!" she exclaimed. "If you need something, I can get it for you. You're supposed to be in bed."

"It's my life," Jack answered tersely. "No matter who or what you are, I can do what I want, so don't try to stop me."

"Mr. Redmond?" The nurse trailed off. His eyes lanced through her.

"Get out of my way," he said, and walked toward her.

"You can't leave here!"

Jack pushed her aside to open the door. She put a hand on his arm. He turned to shove her away. When she fell backward, her head connected with the corner of the small bedside table and her body went still.

Jack moved swiftly out the door and down the hall. Another nurse called out to him. Jack broke into a run. Two of the medical staff emerged from one door on the left side of the hall. Jack almost bowled them over as he raced to the end of the hallway and disappeared around the corner.

In the room that had been Jack Redmond's, the nurse lay motionless. Her blood seeped across the cold floor.

II: The Robert Brennan Memoirs

Flying objects bombarded the police cruiser. A beer bottle shattered against the side-view mirror. Shouts sounded from the group, cursing and threatening. Their rivals fled at the sight of the police vehicle. The rest turned their animosity on the lone police officer.

Officer Brennan threw the door open and hopped out with his pistol in hand. From behind the door, his shield from the mob, he prepared to fire.

"Stop!" he shouted. It would only be a matter of time until backup arrived, but for now, he had to confront the situation alone.

Several in the group rushed toward his vehicle. Brennan leaned into the open to take aim. He fired a shot. Someone returned fire. Some in the approaching group had drawn guns.

Bullets flew everywhere. The scene was a blur. The bullets riddled Brennan's body. The gun fell from his weakened grasp. The hard ground rushed up to meet him...

His eyes snapped open. In a cold sweat, he leaned over to take up his silver pen.

Officer Brennan's pen worked fiercely on the notepad. His writing was fluid and flawless. He always kept his fine silver pen fresh with ink and focused on his penmanship because he knew he couldn't afford to make a mistake.

He often woke like this, rushing to fill the pages and extricate every detail from the unidentifiable blot of quivering gibberish in his brain. It would disperse from him entirely if he didn't write it down.

Once finished, he laid the pen in the passenger's seat and released a sigh. The dream had become a fleeting memory, but he would not forget its underlying reminder of the incident which had spawned his transformation.

Before that occurrence, Brennan had been one of the best officers on the force. Though he had remained absorbed in his work most of the time, he knew it was merely another method of holding his demons at bay. He often deluded himself into believing he wanted to die in the line of duty because it was an honorable way out. In the deep, hidden truths within the folds of his mind, his demons lurked and whispered contradictory chants.

He wanted to embrace the everlasting night, to delve into fathomless eternity. He detested this world's imperfections, and in particular humankind's failures.

The world was prey to uncertainty, existing in a fog of gray. The law was black and white.

He had lived to uphold the law, his securest rein on reality, until that day he had almost slipped into the grave. He then began to sense another law, a greater law, one of consciousness. He came to understand his obligation in pursing this calling if he ever meant to find peace of mind and the ultimate truth he desired.

He had torn the wrinkled paper in places, but it bore his handwriting and in it he expected to see more of the jumbled insanity he had struggled to decipher in the past. Instead, he saw only an address.

368 Greenway Avenue, it read. He dropped the note into the passenger's seat and began the drive across town. He knew the street. He could locate the exact address soon enough.

After he turned onto the street, Officer Brennan received the call from dispatch. The location was dead on. This call would be his to answer, he knew, as he had already arrived on location. He drove along Greenway Avenue until his eyes locked on the gold numbering of *368* above the large house's front door.

III: The Testament of Julia Redmond

The phone rang. Julia sat up on one side of the bed, her feet brushing the fine carpet, and she took the phone from its receiver.

"Hello?" she answered and glanced at the clock. It was eleven–thirty–one.

"Julia Redmond?"

"Yes?" Julia responded with a note of impatience.

"Is your husband there?"

"Who is this?"

"This is Dr. West from the hospital," the voice elaborated. "Your husband left the hospital tonight, and I feel I need to warn you—we don't believe he's exactly stable."

"What do you mean?" Julia asked. Her brow furrowed. She stood from the bed to pace the room in her silky blue nightgown.

"Tonight he suddenly left the hospital and attacked a nurse on his way out."

"He *what?*" Julia exclaimed, incredulous. "Jack isn't always the easiest person to get along with, I'll give you that, but he isn't a violent man. Are you sure it was him?"

"We're positive. We don't know where he is at the moment, but I have a feeling he might try to come by there. I know he's your husband, but be careful. Don't be surprised if the police show up. They've already been here, and a report was filed."

"The police?"

"About the incident with the nurse. She's in intensive care, on life support, as we speak. Your husband needs help. I hate to ask you this, but if he shows up there, try to stall him until the police arrive. He needs treatment, treatment no one can give him until he's found and taken into custody."

"You're saying Jack is crazy? And that he tried to kill someone?" Julia shook her head, switching the phone to her other hand.

"As I said, I know he's your husband, and I'm sure you know him better than anyone, but trust me on this. He may not be the same man you remember."

Julia heard the unmistakable sound of the home's front door opening. Footsteps followed. She looked toward the bedroom door. A knot of fear formed in her stomach.

"Mrs. Redmond?"

"I'll call you back," Julia whispered, and hung up.

She moved down the hall toward the staircase which led down to the living room. Jack stood at the bottom of the stairs, still dressed in the hospital gown. He looked blankly up at her. Her heart skipped a beat. She stepped back.

"I'm home early," Jack said, and began his walk up the stairs. Julia retreated another step.

He paused. "What's wrong?" he asked her. "Is someone here?"

"No," she answered with a bit of confusion and apprehension. "Why would there be? Jack, tell me what's going on. Dr. West called here asking about you."

"I couldn't stay there a minute longer." Jack stopped to wipe the sweat from his brow. His fingers brushed the large bandage encompassing his head. Julia forced herself to remain calm as he again moved toward her, then past her to the bedroom.

"I think you should go back to the hospital," Julia ventured, following him.

She had another thought of the doctor's words, that Jack had assaulted a nurse and she was now barely hanging onto life. He had implied that Jack might have hostile intentions, but despite the severity of what had happened, Julia sensed none of this from her husband. His demeanor did seem strange, but he was still the same man she had known and loved for years, wasn't he?

Jack's next move yanked Julia's fear back to the surface. He opened the drawer of the night stand and took out his pistol.

"Jack," Julia breathed, wide-eyed. She watched him check the chambers of the revolver to make certain the weapon was loaded. His bandaged head turned to look at her, his expression grave.

"Don't worry, honey," he said to her. "Please. I just—" He stopped in mid-sentence. They both heard the vehicle pulling up outside the house.

Jack parted the curtains and looked out the window to the police car parked in the driveway below.

"The police are here?" he asked. Julia blanched.

"I had a feeling someone would be here eventually," Jack admitted.

"Jack, it's true, the police are here for you," Julia said. "Listen to me. You have to give yourself up. You can't run from the police. It's going to be okay, babe, I promise. Just please, don't do anything crazy."

Jack didn't answer. He gripped the revolver and took another glance out the window.

"Just promise me, Jack."

The doorbell rang. Julia strode out of the bedroom. To her relief, Jack remained inside. She shut the door behind her and went downstairs. She could only hope nothing more would come of this.

"Mrs. Redmond," the pale police officer greeted her at the front door, his features glistening under a sheen of sweat. "I'm Officer Brennan. Is Mr. Redmond at home?"

"I..." she faltered.

"I see." A knowing expression crossed Officer Brennan's features. He clearly read the quandary in Julia's hesitation. "Mind if I have a look around?"

"Please, I don't want anything to happen," Julia pleaded in a low voice.

"I understand," he said. "I'll just have a look around." She opened the door further to allow entry. He came into the house.

"Does your husband have a penchant for violent behavior?" he asked. He walked the length of the home's bottom level.

"Jack wouldn't hurt a fly," Julia said. "I really don't understand what's going on."

"Mind if I take a look upstairs?" Brennan inquired. Julia swallowed, uncertain. He noted her reaction without comment and proceeded up the stairs.

"He's in the bedroom," Julia confessed in a whisper. "Please, I don't want anything bad to happen. I just want my husband to be the man I married, the man he was before this happened to him."

"I understand, Mrs. Redmond," Brennan said to her, "but I'm going to have to ask you to stay downstairs."

Julia watched with fear as Officer Brennan moved to the top of the stairs and down the hall toward the bedroom. His hand rested on his pistol. He reached the door, placed a hand on the door knob, and gave it a slow turn.

A moment later, he stood level with Jack Redmond's gun. Jack opened fire.

Julia screamed. Blood and gray matter rained onto the floor. Brennan dropped. Jack emptied every round into his body until the pistol clicked with emptied chambers.

He looked up at nothing in particular and held his gun aloft. "Your messenger is dead," he declared. "I am not yours in this life!" He stepped over the dead officer's body.

"Jack," Julia whispered in horror.

She scrambled past him toward the bedroom. When she reached the doorway, she halted and looked back. Could it be true that Jack had just murdered an officer of the law in their own home? She couldn't believe it and could hardly even think now.

She darted into the bedroom. She would call the police, she decided. Would her husband be shut away in prison for the rest of his days? Would he be put away in some mental institution to rot forever? Would he face execution? She didn't know, but she had to do something.

She grabbed the phone and contacted the operator. She asked

to speak to the police and frantically insisted it was an emergency. Her breath left her when she saw Jack standing at the door. The phone fell from her grasp. Jack pointed the gun at her.

"Calling the police on me?" Jack asked. Julia gasped.

"Hang up the phone," Jack said.

"I'm your wife!" she blurted. Tears welled forth. She stared at her husband in disbelief.

"You don't understand what's happening," Jack said to her. He reached up to scratch the side of his head through the bandage.

"I don't," Julia said, lowering her head. "For the love of God, Jack, I don't understand it at all. All I know is that you need help, Jack. You need professional help. Please let me call someone. You don't need the gun."

"No one can help me but me," Jack said. "Listen. I want you to understand—but I wouldn't know where to begin. I saw something, Julia, something terrible. I saw the truth. I saw the truth about who and what I am and what I always was."

"What?" Julia asked.

"Have you ever considered the possibility that some of us, possibly even all of us, may be damned from the beginning, that our lives are only a brief delay from a terrible storm the likes of which we can never know in mortal life?"

"That's not true, Jack," Julia said.

"Something is waiting for me on the other side, Julia. I have seen it!"

"You're acting crazy!" Julia cried. The image of her husband seized by such maniacal delusions stung her tear-filled eyes. "That blow to the head did something to you—"

Julia stopped as something caught her attention, an image in the hallway beyond where Jack stood.

What Julia saw in that moment would plunge her vision into currents of darkness. Julia, in her years of incessant wide-eyed mumbling and crazed banter to follow, would become lost in the hazy recesses of her own self-perpetuated shell of madness. She would relive the terror time and time again for the rest of her days.

Jack saw the color flush from her face as she stared past him. He turned to look into the hall.

The corpse of Officer Brennan rose. Its eyes looked through Jack. Brennan's eyes were the eyes of the void, dead eyes, but they held a knowing glint. The grin upon Brennan's open face, covered in blood and speckled with bits of his own skull and nervous tissue, was inhuman.

Brennan opened fire. Jack sprawled to the carpeted floor. Julia screamed.

The gunfire desisted. Julia ran across the room to her husband.

She watched Jack's blood soak into the carpet, the first thought in her turbulent mind to call an ambulance, yet elsewhere within the turmoil, she knew an ambulance would never arrive in time.

Brennan's lifeless corpse sank to the floor. Jack's words repeated themselves in Julia's mind before the dark currents swept her away.

She stared into the fractured channels of death. A cosmic balance had tipped by orchestrations of a nether-black chaos which mortals could never know, and as their lives were but grains of sand spiraling through the whirlwind, Jack Redmond and Officer Robert Brennan had served as mere tools for their parasitic master's manipulation.

Julia could only sob hysterically. For the rest of her years to follow, her husband's tortured screams would resound throughout her darkest nightmares, screams to echo mutely throughout eternity from beyond the void of oblivion.

Contessa

I: Departures

In her childhood, Stacey Whatley was like many other children in that an inherent magic existed in much of the world to her, in its sights and sounds, colors, shapes, and the curiosity it fostered in a ripe, remarkable imagination with boundaries unknown. With age and experience came disillusionment. Dreams were crushed and magic was forgotten in a life that tolerated neither until Stacey's unexpected rediscovery, courtesy of a pen and paper and a man named Raphael Gettyson.

Before she read Gettyson's work, Stacey hated poetry. The difference in Gettyson's work was its curious familiarity to her, that as she devoured page after page, she began to remember, returning to a forgotten window of her early childhood. She unlearned the rigid teachings that had come to bind her perceptions and could again appreciate the truths written in nature, the universe, and its beauty.

When she closed the poetry book and looked around, she observed a place where appreciation was virtually absent and the rules for life, views, and personality were dictated by society's views, which were in turn sculpted by the media and authoritarian figures pushing an agenda involving money, control, or both.

Gettyson's poetry volume was the catalyst for liberation. Stacey Whatley stood on the shores of an island of the Mediterranean, her new beginning.

Her bare feet in the sand, she looked to the ocean. Waves of blue and aqua-foam rushed forward to meet her open embrace. She looked into the water, into the sand, into the skies, into the cosmos. Of it, her senses drank in exhilaration.

Later, while sprawled on her luxury chair, drinking fresh coffee and smoking a hookah with one of her newfound friends, she made another life-changing discovery. Her friend handed two thin poetry volumes back to her without a word.

"And?" Stacey prompted.

Her friend shrugged. Stacey persisted. "Really? No opinion whatsoever?"

"It is good, I suppose," the friend replied.

"Just good?"

The friend gave another shrug. With a sigh, Stacey reached for her blue-and-green patterned ceramic cup and took a tentative sip of steamy black coffee.

"If not for Raphael Gettyson," Stacey said, "I wouldn't be here today." She clinked her cup back down on the small, hexagonal glass table beside her. "And we wouldn't be having this conversation." Her friend leaned over, took a long pull on the hookah, clouds of peachy smoke puffing upward, and offered it to Stacey. Stacey took it, rested her lips against the mouthpiece, and drew in the flavorful smoke.

"I did look up some background information," her friend said. "I was curious."

"Oh?" Stacey responded, finishing her smoke. She passed the hose back to her friend.

She took the hose Stacey offered and drew in another round of smoke. She exhaled, a light cloud billowing gently into the air, and spoke again. "They say he is not long for this world."

"Gettyson?" Stacey sat up a bit. She seldom even considered the man himself, despite his poetry having impacted her to such a degree.

"It is believed he is ill," the friend said, "that he may soon pass away. It is doubtful there will ever be a third poetry volume, unless it had already been written and remains unshared."

"Where did you find this information?" Stacey asked. The friend just shook her head and passed the hookah hose back over.

As she smoked, Stacey considered possibilities she had never entertained, including that of unread verses from the pen of Raphael Gettyson.

"If you would like," her friend said, "I can show you."

Stacey took another puff from the hookah and watched the smoke float in spiral layers around the room. She inclined her head to look at the ceiling, into the smoky spiral's pinnacle, and watched it dance. During that short span of precious time, she made her decision.

"I would like that," she answered. Tomorrow, Stacey decided, she would begin her search for Raphael Gettyson.

II: Departure

To Stacey's fortune, her friend's connections proved useful. She had a habit of conducting research for the sake of pure curiosity and didn't mind assisting Stacey in her search for Raphael Gettyson.

There seemed to be no detailed information about the man. The publisher of Raphael's poetry books was a small press that had gone under years before, at which time Gettyson's works became out-of-print. After plumbing what information she could about the company, Stacey found only one name associated with it, the company's owner prior to its liquidation.

Stacey looked at the telephone. Did she dare take it to the next level?

After a moment of staring at the phone, she dialed the number.

"Hello?"

"Hello. Is Mr. Parker home?"

"Is this a cruel joke? Who are you?"

"What? No. I—"

"My husband has been dead for years."

Stacey fell silent. She regretted making the call.

"Hello?" spoke the elderly female voice from the phone.

"I'm sorry," Stacey said. "I had no idea."

"It's all right." The voice had softened. "But it's been years. You didn't know? Who are you and why are you looking for my husband?"

"His company published two books of poetry by a man named Raphael Gettyson."

"Ah," the woman's voice answered. "Yes?"

"I've heard that Raphael Gettyson was ill. I wanted to—well, you could say I wanted to speak to him. His poetry meant a lot to me. It still does, really. Maybe I just wanted him to know how much his work affected me."

"I see." The woman didn't speak for almost a minute, but Stacey heard paper ruffling, pages turning, and then the older woman spoke again. "This is the best I can do: I have the contact address and phone number of his editor. Will that work?"

"It'll have to," Stacey said. "I'll take whatever you have. I appreciate this."

"Do you have a pen?"

"Right here."

The woman relayed the address and phone number. Stacey wrote it down and thanked her. Once off the phone, Stacey made another phone call, now to Gettyson's editor of years ago.

She could feel herself getting closer. A woman answered the telephone after the third ring.

"Hello?"

"Is this Eileen Northrop?"

"Who is this?"

"This is Stacey Whatley. I'm trying to find the editor of two poetry volumes by a man named Raphael Gettyson."

"Where did you find this number?"

Stacey sighed into the receiver with audible exasperation and caught herself too late. The woman spoke again, but her tone, instead of irritated or dismissive as Stacey feared, became calm and slightly less inquisitive.

"Yes, this is Eileen Northrop. Who is this, and what do you need?"

Stacey introduced herself and stated the reason for her call. Eileen listened in silence until she finished.

"I can't release personal information," Eileen said, "and that includes personal contact information."

"There must be some way you can help me. Please?"

Stacey almost thought she heard a muffled chuckle on the line's other end. After a moment, Eileen said, "I'll have to check my records."

Her tone had lightened, but there remained a dubious note. "That was years ago, you have to understand. I can't guarantee I'll have anything."

"Anything you can do will help me," Stacey said.

"Can you give me a number to reach you?"

Stacey gave Eileen the number. Minutes later the phone rested on its receiver, quiet. To pass the time, Stacey smoked her hookah, but this time by herself. The thick smoke swirled around the room until she set the hookah aside, reclined, and fell asleep.

Hours into her slumber, the phone rang. Stacey woke in a confused daze before remembering her earlier phone calls. She snatched up the phone. It was Eileen Northrop, to her surprise. She admitted to herself that she hadn't really expected Eileen to return her call at all, much less this quickly.

"You're lucky, you know," Eileen said. "I have all of the old records in storage. I meant to get rid of them, but keep missing the opportunity. I did find a number and an address, but that isn't information I can disclose. I made some calls on my own, however." A stretch of silence followed.

"Yes?" Stacey ventured.

"The address I have doesn't hold up," Eileen said. "The Gettysons don't live there anymore. But I managed to contact Meyer Gettyson and I explained your interest to him. If it suits you, he has agreed to speak with you."

"*Meyer* Gettyson?"

"His brother."

"What about Raphael?"

"He's unavailable." Eileen Northrop left it at this. Stacey's mind churned possibilities. Was Raphael Gettyson too ill? Had he already passed on?

Eileen hadn't said this, of course. Wouldn't she have if it was the case?

"Ms. Whatley?" Eileen said.

"Sorry. Yes, I'll speak with him. I have a pen right here, whenever you're ready to give me the number."

"I don't have a phone number for you."

"Pardon?"

"I only have an address. The impression I'm given is that, if you want to speak with Mr. Gettyson, you'll need to do it in person."

"Why?"

Impatience entered Eileen's tone. "Do you want the address?"

"Yes," Stacey said. "I'm ready." She took down the address as Eileen gave it to her and murmured her thanks into the receiver. After hanging up the phone, she stared at the piece of paper. She had no idea it would lead to this. She didn't even live in the United States anymore. Now, on a whim, she was supposed to travel across the globe to speak with someone she had never met about a poetry book? She had the address, so why couldn't she just send a letter?

This would take a lot of thinking about. She set the piece of paper aside and made a drink.

With her fresh glass of brandy, cherries, and cream, along with her hookah and comfortable reclining chair, Stacey relaxed for the next hour, but her eyes kept returning to the table beside her where the slip of paper lay. The longer she looked at the address written on it, the more she had to acknowledge that Gettyson's poetry truly *had* changed her life.

The old Stacey would never have considered it, but the Stacey of today knew that, despite her comfortable arrangement here, the address would lead her from the Mediterranean and back across the world to the United States Midwest where her destination of the Gettyson home awaited.

III: Arrival

After Stacey secured her hotel room at the Chandling, she threw a few items into her bag, one of them a canister of pepper spray, and slung the bag around her shoulder. She climbed onto her bicycle to begin her ride out of the city limits. She stopped to study a map before making her way down city streets and eventually to the outskirts.

For almost a half-hour she rolled by fields of green, her trip marked by the occasional house, until she realized she was almost there. She rolled past the white fence to the edge of a driveway occupied by a gray sedan. Stacey checked her address with that of the white square house, ensuring it matched. She parked her bicycle across from it and paused to catch her breath after the long ride.

She walked to the door. Since it featured no doorbell, she knocked. Not long after, the door opened. A young man with dark, pronounced features, mid-thirties perhaps, modestly dressed, stood in front of her.

"Hello," he greeted, his voice containing an inquisitive note, but warm. He glanced at the bicycle outside and showed the trace of a smile.

"You rode that thing over here?"

Stacey nodded. The man gave a slight eyebrow-raised nod, but moved on to an introduction. "I'm Meyer Gettyson. You must be Stacey."

She nodded again. He stepped away from the door.

"Come in," he said.

Stacey entered a sea-toned room with a cushy chair, sofa and loveseat, and a glass coffee table reminiscent of the one she had left behind in another part of the world. Meyer motioned for her to have a seat. She sat on the edge of the sofa. Meyer walked to a doorway which led into an adjoining room—the kitchen, it appeared from where Stacey sat.

He stopped at the doorway. "Something to drink?" he asked.

Stacey could smell coffee. After a moment's hesitation, she said, "If you're making coffee, I might have a cup."

"Certainly. Cream? Sugar?"

"No, thank you."

"That's good," Meyer replied amiably, "because I don't keep any here."

Meyer disappeared into the kitchen. Stacey's eyes roamed the living room until he returned to place a hot mug of black coffee in her hands.

Meyer took a seat in the room's single chair, positioned diagonally from the sofa. He blew across the top of his coffee to cool it and took a sip.

"So you like my brother's poetry," Meyer said.

"It means a lot to me." After she said it, the statement sounded banal to her, silly even, but Meyer nodded, though his expression remained neutral. He held his coffee up to take another sip, deeper than the first.

"It must, if you wanted to come all this way," he said. "I talked to Eileen, as you know. She said it was strange, your calling her, but that you seemed genuine."

"I would like to speak to him," Stacey said. "That is, if I could. I heard something about a health condition. Is your brother well?"

After Stacey spoke, her delivery struck her as awkward. Now that she sat here speaking with Raphael Gettyson's own brother, Stacey couldn't be certain of the proper way to proceed.

She still had no idea of whether the news of the man's illness had been accurate or whether she would find him here. Only Meyer had met her here as of yet and he had offered nothing to Stacey of his brother.

Meyer's smile was simple and, she thought, kind and uncritical. He leaned back, making himself comfortable before speaking again, but instead of answering her question, he asked a question of his own.

"Would you mind telling me your story?"

Stacey began to describe her discovery of his brother's poetry, though she had difficulty describing exactly how it had affected her. For lack of a sufficient explanation, she just pushed forward with the story.

She related her travel to her new home in the Mediterranean and how profoundly different, better, life had been to her at that point, but what had seemed incredible then sounded like mindless self-indulgence now. She glanced toward Meyer, but he stared down at his coffee.

She decided not to carry it on for much longer. She had heard that Raphael Gettyson was in poor health, she explained, and that news had brought her here. That was the truth, but the story didn't yet have an ending because of the question left hanging in the room's silence, the unanswered question Stacey had earlier asked. *Is your brother well?*

"When he wrote his first collection of poetry," Meyer said, still looking at his coffee, "on scraps of paper and whatever he could find, I never thought anything would come of it. A lot of people write poetry. And in the end, so what?

"When our mother was sick in the hospital, the doctors didn't give her a chance. A few days at most, they said. The nurses did anything they could to make her as comfortable as possible. I visited as often as I could. Raphael stayed by her side and read his poetry to her while she slept. Somehow, she recovered. Just like that. Not long after, she left the hospital, better than ever. She went on for another ten years, in fact.

"In her sleep, our mother had heard my brother's poetry. She believed it had saved her. I didn't believe any such thing. My mother believed it, though, and so did the others she convinced. That's where the story really began. That's what first created such an interest in my brother's poetry and led to his first poetry book, *Contessa.* Contessa was our mother's name, you see.

"Years later, well after he had written *Contessa* and then *Waking,* his publisher folded. Later in the same year, our mother passed away. I never saw my brother write any more poetry after that. Things changed, and he left."

Meyer took a drink of his coffee. Stacey shook her head, a tad confused.

"But what happened?" she asked. "Where is he? Do you still talk to him?"

Meyer's eyes met Stacey's. He leaned on the thick, plush arm of his chair. "I don't know what happened, to be honest." His eyes slipped down to the coffee cup again. Stacey fumbled in her mind for something to ask, some suitable question, but Meyer spared her the effort.

"When I really saw the change in him," he said, "or when I was no longer able to deny it, it was not long after our mother died. A pipe in our basement burst. After we had it repaired, Raphael and I went down into the basement to take care of the mess and salvage what we could. Most of it was ruined by then, but in one of the soggy old cardboard boxes, he found his old personal copy of *Contessa.* That's when things got worse.

"You heard my brother was ill, you said. To be frank, he was always a bit ill, but after I saw him huddling there in the basement, shaking and holding that wet, ruined copy of his first poetry volume, I knew something had changed. When he looked at me, it was as if he didn't even recognize me, his own brother. Over the days and weeks after that, he became sullen and distant and barely ever said anything. One day, he left."

There it was again, that phrase. *He left.* Before Stacey could dissect that one tiny, simple statement, she observed a change in Meyer's demeanor, a slight downturn at the edges of his lips and a darkening of his eyes, cast at the carpet now.

"Is that all?" Stacey asked, and winced at these words, again feeling she couldn't communicate her meaning with accuracy. She wanted to reassure Meyer, comfort him, but she felt she had only brought him more misery with her questions and her presence here, which must remind him of the brother he had lost. If

Raphael Gettyson still lived, however, even if ill, was the situation beyond hope? Surely not.

When Meyer looked up at her, she realized with a flush of embarrassment that she had been staring. She looked away.

Meyer sighed. "That's all I can tell you. I know you came a long way. I'm sorry I couldn't be of more help."

"It's okay," Stacey said. "I'm glad you were willing to see me and tell me the things you did."

He swirled his coffee in its cup, silent and thoughtful. Eventually, he raised his gaze to her again. "Where are you staying?"

"The Chandling Hotel."

"I know the place. Do you need a ride into the city? Or would you rather hop back onto that bike, the same way you got here?" The faint smile returned to his features. Stacey involuntarily shared the smile in her own fashion. She almost told him not to bother, that she was fine on her own, but at the last second, a different answer emerged.

"Sure, I'll take a ride. Thank you."

Outside, Meyer lifted her bicycle and maneuvered it into the trunk of his car. He set it down with care. After he closed the trunk, the two climbed into the car. Meyer started the engine.

"Buckle up," he said. Stacey clicked the seat belt into place and Meyer kicked the car into reverse. He backed it onto the road and launched them up the long stretch.

IV: In Memoriam

Meyer kept both hands on the wheel, his eyes fixed on the road ahead, and he said little. His casual brand of warmth from before had placed her at ease, but this accomplished the opposite. She shifted in her seat and looked out the passenger's side window.

She recalled something Meyer had said about his brother. *He was always a bit ill.* He hadn't elaborated, but it made her wonder.

Meyer drove through the city, through bustling traffic beneath brown and gray buildings, and pulled up to a stoplight. He stared straight ahead until the light turned green, and they began moving again. They neared the block of Stacey's hotel. Meyer gave no signs of slowing when they neared the turn for it.

"Right here," Stacey indicated, and pointed to the right where the street turned away. Meyer passed it.

"The turn was back there," Stacey said. When the car ahead of them slowed to a halt and Meyer stopped to wait for the next traffic light to change, he looked over at Stacey.

"I said before that I had told you all I could tell you. For the most part, that's true, but I've been thinking a lot in the short time since we've met and since you told me your story. You came this far. My brother's poetry really meant that much to you, did it?"

"It changed my life."

With a hesitant nod, Meyer gauged his next words before speaking again. "Maybe there's something you should see."

"I'm not sure I follow," Stacey said. "But, okay."

For a second, a flash of Meyer's former smile returned. "Okay," he said. He drove on without saying anything else. He seemed tense, troubled, but Stacey made a conscious effort to refrain from questioning his strange behavior until they reached their destination.

The buildings were older in this part of the city. Trash littered the street. A number of unkempt vagrants stared from the sidewalks. When the car stopped at the next traffic light, someone tapped on the passenger's side window, startling Stacey.

"Got change?" a large, red-faced man with a greasy beard asked. Stacey shook her head quickly. The light turned green. Meyer drove on. The bearded man gawked after them.

A group of young men watched them, their eyes hard, but Meyer's continued acceleration left them behind. Farther along, he turned down a side road. He drove until they reached the next turn and slowed the car. This area appeared dim, as much of the sunlight seemed obscured by the closeness of the box-block buildings clustered around them.

Meyer pulled the car to one side. Stacey cast him a sideways glance, wondering whether it was sane to stop here. Meyer answered her by gesturing toward a dark, narrow alleyway ahead, on the left.

"There," he said to her. He betrayed no expression. Her eyes quizzical, Stacey looked out the window again and climbed halfway out of the vehicle before turning back to him. He sat there, hands on the wheel, still looking ahead.

"Are you coming?" Stacey asked. He shook his head. Stacey shrugged. She closed the door.

The air smelled of gasoline and old refuse. A light breeze stirred crumpled pieces of paper on the concrete.

"Well, let's do this," Stacey said to herself. She walked to the alleyway.

Even during the day, the downtown alley carved a thin stretch of night through the city's underbelly. Stacey walked into the narrow space between walls of mottled brick. Along the alley, she saw only the garbage that strewed the ground and graffiti sprayed in yellow, white, and gold across the walls on each side of her. At the opposite end of the alley, past the place where this alley intersected with another, a mound of garbage had spilled from an overturned can. She caught a sour smell in the air.

Why had Meyer sent her this way?

She wasn't looking deep enough. She hadn't looked in the right place.

This she realized when the words of Raphael's poetry flowed through her mind, the volumes of *Contessa* and *Waking* that had become such a part of her life. Through this she recognized the poetry of Raphael Gettyson written in spray paint across the alleyway walls, though it was not the Raphael Gettyson whose works she had known and cherished.

It was the Raphael Gettyson who had held a putrefied poetry volume in a dank basement, trembling, the man who had watched his mother leave this world even as he gave her everything of himself and saw that it would not save her. It was the Raphael Gettyson who saw his world crumbling and the pages of his poetry's beauty withered, yellowed, and fading, the paths to ruin leading in every direction and an unspoken promise of destitution upon the silence.

Stacey Whatley stood in the alleyway, reading the words of Raphael Gettyson's third and final volume in yellow, white, and gold on brick, and it seemed fitting that the world would only know two volumes.

To her mild surprise, she found Meyer standing in wait for her at the alley's entrance. She looked at him, grateful he had come, but said nothing.

Meyer's dark eyes were resigned. "Let's just go," he said, and turned away. Stacey touched his shoulder.

From that refuse pile at the other end of the alley, something stirred.

"What is it?" Meyer asked Stacey, turning back toward her. She shook her head and took a couple of small steps back to the alley's opening. Though she saw only the defiled alleyway and the garbage littering it, she could feel eyes on her. Before she left with Meyer, she uttered her words of farewell to anyone who might hear.

"Thank you," she said.

Orchard Girls

I: Aqua Vitae

Morty held the aluminum baseball bat in the summer sun. The scuffmarks on its surface shone like metallic victory notches. Big Sparky, he had called the lucky slugger since his younger days, when he slammed many a home run into the stratosphere.

He tossed the ball upward and swung. A metallic flash, a crack, and the ball was gone.

Morty held a hand above his eyes to shield them from the sunlight and searched for the ball. It was amazing, like back in his youth, or even better!

He picked up the bottle in the grass and peered at the clear liquid inside it. *Aqua vitae* was scrawled on its makeshift label, a worn strip of yellow masking tape.

After his first small sip, Morty had felt like the king of the world. He began to question his original skepticism about the stories his grandfather had told him, tales of the Spring of Life which flowed through every world, and that yarn about his grandparents having lived for over two hundred years.

Sunlight glinted through the quarter-filled bottle of water. Could it be true that his grandfather really had discovered that incredible spring?

"All sorts of funny flying creatures," his grandfather had said to his grandmother. "Sparkly as a fireworks show. And a little creature with three horns, like a dinosaur, a miniature version of a triceratops like you might in the children's books—I saw it drinking from the spring, too. I knew this had to be something special!"

His grandfather's head jerked around when Morty wandered in on his little toddler legs. Both of his grandparents stared at him. His grandfather held the bottle: *aqua vitae.*

They forbid Morty to touch it in his younger days, but after his grandparents passed on to the next world, leaving him with this large stretch of property and the bottle, he wondered.

When he drank from it, to his astonishment, he felt uplifted, powerful, and he realized the things his grandfather had said about that spring had to be real. What else could this water do?

Later, while he sat in front of his coffee table, absently looking at the large brown fruit bowl on its surface, an interesting idea trickled into his thoughts. All this land, Morty thought, passed down to me along with the magical water. The land would be perfect for farming, wouldn't it? If the water had extended his grandparents' lifespan and supported forms of life unknown to the rest of this world, what would it accomplish if he used it to grow vegetables or fruit?

An orchard. Yes!

The next day, he went out to purchase everything he would need. Lemons and oranges, he decided, and to begin with, he would only use a single drop of this miracle fluid and wait to see what happened.

With a shiny new shovel Morty dug the holes, four of them, while he allowed the tiny trees to soak for a few hours before lowering them into the ground. He planted three orange trees and one lemon tree. He would start small. Who knew how much work an entire orchard would be? Not Morty. Not yet, at least.

He patted the soil down, secured each of the trees, and added a drop of the water of life to each. He left his supplies on the ground, taking only the bottle of aqua vitae with him, and went home to have a pimento cheese sandwich and a beer. After two more beers and a stand-up comedy television special that did little but confuse him, he decided to stay home, but made a note to check on the trees tomorrow afternoon.

When he returned to the site of his first four trees, they were taller than him! The trunks were beginning to fill out.

He whistled. This was really something.

The next day, the trees grew even more, towering overhead to yield gigantic bunches of sizable oranges and lemons. Had he accidentally planted grapefruits instead of oranges? The lemons were equally huge, though. It had to be the magical water at work.

He picked one of the oranges and went home again. He plunked the large orange onto the counter and cut it into slices. He bit into the juicy pulp. Orange sweetness filled his mouth. It was juicy, refreshing, and easily the best orange Morty had ever tasted!

He would bring baskets tomorrow and gather what lemons and oranges he had room for in his pickup truck. There were a lot of them, and as large as they were, he had a good amount of work ahead of him.

"And just imagine how much I could get from a full orchard?" he mused aloud.

The next day, he parked his truck near the trees and carried the stacked baskets out to the fruit trees to gather what he could. When he arrived, the baskets slipped from his grasp and bounced on the ground. He stood gaping.

Beneath each of the trees, a small girl lay curled up, sleeping—two girls with heaps of orange hair on their heads and a yellow-haired girl at the base of the lemon tree. A green cord, like a stem or a vine, connected each of the girls to her respective tree by her stomach.

The girl beneath the lemon tree sat up, rubbed against the tree trunk, and noticed Morty. She looked at him sleepily and wiped her eyes. When her eyes opened wider, Morty saw her irises were as yellow as her hair—lemon-yellow. Seconds later, the orange girls rolled around and stirred, waking in a similar manner.

Morty's grandfather's tales of the Spring of Life's mystical creatures ran through his whirling mind. With the combination of the spring's magical waters and a few fruit trees, he realized, he had brought these bizarre creatures into being!

The girls continued to watch him. He tried speaking to them.

"Hi," he said. None of the girls responded. They kept staring.

They answered Morty's initial efforts to communicate with blank looks. Eventually one of the orange girls opened her mouth to make a sound, but nonsensical sounds emerged. Morty tried another approach.

"Morty," he said, pointing at himself. "Morty."

"Mor—Morty," the lemon girl repeated, her speech slow and uncertain. She rolled her tongue around in her mouth. "Morty?"

Soon, the orange girls repeated it. "Morty."

Morty began the long process of conveying simple words and associating them with meanings.

"Stay." He used this to keep them here, right near their trees. Once they understood, he moved on.

"Home," he attempted next. They watched with interest, but he wasn't sure how much they could understand.

"Home," he repeated, pointing to the orchard girls, and then to the trees. He pointed into the distance, where his truck waited. He started to walk. When he turned, he saw the girls having difficulty breaking free from their trees.

He returned to cut them free. "I don't know if this will hurt or not," he said. "I hope not." He withdrew his pocketknife and cut the stems. The girls didn't react. Once he had severed the stems, Morty led the girls away and this time they followed him back to his truck.

"Home," they all chimed.

Morty walked around to the back of the truck and opened the tailgate. "In you go," he said. They stood unmoving, so he gently helped them into its bed.

"Stay," he said.

When he started the engine and took off, he glanced in the mirror and saw the girls still sitting there, the wind blowing in their wild hair.

Good, he thought. Maybe none of them will try to jump out.

He drove across the field, bound for home with a truckload of magically grown orchard girls.

II: When Life Hands You Lemons and Oranges

The girls' lips were a vivid orange and yellow, as were their tongues. Their skin held a tinge of the same color. These details and more Morty noticed as the days whished past.

After a week, the orchard girls adapted to Morty's small house. They watched a lot of television but ate nothing from the refrigerator. They did drink a lot of water, and often went outdoors to stretch out on towels in the grass and bask in the warm sunlight. Morty insisted they use the back door for their sunbathing, not wanting his odd new discovery to be lounging around out front and drawing attention.

Mentally, they developed to a startling degree over the next few weeks. Their vocabulary increased. Other than what they learned from Morty, they mostly gleaned it from television, but at least they were making progress, and on a level that, for a human child, would have been unbelievable.

The aspects of their physical maturation stunned Morty even more. He watched, amazed, as the girls blossomed into womanhood. They walked around his living room, shameless slender girls with firm breasts bobbing.

"So, um, we were thinking," one of the orange girls said one day to Morty, "can you buy us some clothes?"

They had to ask sooner or later. Morty sighed with reluctance, but he agreed. His bank account shrank. Soon the girls wrapped themselves in clothing they had selected from various department store catalogs.

"What about some jewelry?" another of the orange girls asked.

"No!" Morty exclaimed. The girl pouted.

"What about makeup?" another orange girl asked to Morty's further exasperation.

"Girls, please," the yellow-haired girl said to the orange girls, "just calm down."

Morty glanced at her. "Thanks, Lemon Girl."

Her yellow lips smiled. "You're welcome!" At least one of them can pretend to be halfway mature, Morty told himself, and went to the refrigerator to grab a beer.

"You only let us go into the back yard," said an orange girl once Morty sat on the couch with his beer. "When do we get to go somewhere else?"

"Not yet," Morty replied, his nerves frayed. "Give me time, okay?" He tried watching television, but to his further annoyance, the girls kept talking over the television.

"Can you please be quiet?" he asked, but they ignored him. After a few more minutes of this, he gave up and retired to the bedroom, grabbing two more beers on the way.

He drank his beer in bed, but heard the girls chattering noisily across the house. He decided he would have to drink himself into a coma in order to get some sleep. When he went back to the refrigerator to get more beer, he ran into Lemon Girl there.

"I'm sorry," she said with a helpless shrug. "It's those orange girls!"

Morty leaned into the refrigerator to take a beer from the back. "What are you drinking?" Lemon Girl asked him. She leaned over the top of the refrigerator door.

"Beer," he said. He twisted the top open and took a hearty guzzle. He saw her watching him and added, "You're not old enough to drink, Lemon Girl."

"I'm almost two months old!" she said. Morty sat at his kitchen table. Lemon Girl sat down across from him.

"Two months isn't old enough," he replied after another drink.

"But I'm just like an adult woman," she argued. "Kind of."

Morty contemplated this. Sure, she was, sort of. She could pass for eighteen, although strange with her yellowish features.

"Do you think I'm pretty?" Lemon Girl asked him.

Morty blinked. "Huh?" He quickly finished his beer.

"Want another one?" Lemon Girl asked. Morty nodded. She fetched him one from the refrigerator and readdressed the subject. "I was asking if you thought I was pretty."

"Well, yeah," Morty said after she handed him the cold beer. "But you're different."

"Different? You mean different from the orange girls or different from regular girls?"

"All of that."

"But that could be a good thing," Lemon Girl said. "Don't you think?"

"I guess. I don't know."

"Do you want to kiss me?"

Morty faltered. He took a quick sip of beer.

"Well?"

With the aid of liquid courage, he leaned forward. Lemon Girl met him halfway across the table. Their lips met. Through the taste of beer, Morty tasted her lips, and after that, her tongue, which tasted lemony.

Lemon Girl stayed close to him after that. She kept bringing him beer throughout the night. When they talked, she leaned close to him and they shared another kiss. After a few more beers, the night became hazy to Morty, and suddenly he was out of beer and under the sheets of his bed with Lemon Girl.

The alcoholic fog faded. Morty's head spun. His stomach roiled. "I think I'm gonna be sick," he said. Lemon Girl looked over at him.

"Sick?" she echoed.

He swallowed it back, although his stomach continued to lurch, and finally he sprang out of bed, rushed to the bathroom, and vomited into the toilet. When he sprawled there with his arms around the porcelain, retching, Lemon Girl stood over him and watched.

"It's okay," she said. "I'll take care of you."

Morty groaned. "Water," he rasped. "That's all I need right now."

"Okay, Morty."

Morty slumped away from the toilet and against the wall. He wiped his mouth with the bathroom towel that had fallen from near the sink. Lemon Girl came back into the small bathroom.

"Here," she said, and held the bottle to his lips. He took a sip and instantly felt better. His drunken sickness subsided as if eliminated by sheer magic. He climbed to his feet.

"Wait," he said, startled when he saw the glass bottle she held. *Aqua vitae*, its label read. "Where did you find this?" He snatched it from her. She flinched.

"The orange girls had it," she said, defensiveness in her tone. "I took it from them. I was afraid they would break it and you would be mad. Why, is it special?"

He held up the bottle. "This is very special, Lemon Girl. This belonged to my grandparents."

"Can I try some?"

Morty glared. "No!"

"What's so special about it?"

"It's—" Morty paused. Should he tell her? He walked out of the bathroom and sat on the edge of the bed. She sat beside him, too close now for his comfort, but the strange, jumbled memories of their earlier roll in the sack prodded him. He shuddered.

"It's what?" she urged. "Come on, Morty, you can tell me."

She would only become more curious if he didn't, Morty guessed, so he tried to explain.

94

"Without this," he said, "you and the other girls wouldn't be here." He proceeded to tell her about the aqua vitae, his grandparents, and the idea of planting an orchard. Lemon Girl clung to his every word. By the time he finished his story, ending with the appearance of the orchard girls beneath the fruit trees, her face loomed close and he could taste her citrusy breath. Her eyes were large, awestruck by the story.

"Wow," she said.

III: Big Sparky

"I don't know how much more of this I can take," Morty muttered.

"Me?" Lemon Girl's voice made Morty wince.

"Them," he said. The orange girls were loud, like they had been the night before, but this morning he wasn't drunk. The water of life had cured any possibility of a hangover, but the girls' manic chattering and squealing still irked him at this early hour of the morning.

"Want me to make them be quiet?" Lemon Girl asked.

"Yeah," Morty said. "Please." He felt the mattress shift when she climbed out of bed. Once she closed the door, he turned his head into the warm pillow. Irritated, he flipped the pillow over and lay against the cooler side of it in an attempt to go back to sleep.

After that, the morning became surprisingly peaceful. How Lemon Girl managed to keep the others in line, he didn't know, but he didn't need to know. It worked.

When Morty climbed out of bed, he went into the kitchen to find a glass of milk and a warm toaster pastry waiting on the table. He looked around. "Lemon Girl, did you do this?"

She smiled at him. "Yes."

"Thanks," he said, and sat down. She sat at the other end of the table. He munched on the toaster pastry, which happened to be lemon-filled, and sipped his milk. Lemon Girl watched him.

"When are you going to show me more?" she asked.

"Show you more?" A mouthful of lemon pastry and milk muffled Morty's reply.

"New things. Like that special bottle of water. Or that thing we did in bed last night. That was fun. I told the other girls about that and they want to try it, too."

Morty almost choked on his food.

"Okay, listen," Morty said once he swallowed down his large bite of breakfast. "I think we should put a hold on everything for now."

"Why?" she asked.

"I need to rest today," he said, "and think."

"Oh," she said, and looked down at the table. "Okay."

The day remained peaceful, and by noon, his mood improved. A quiet house made all the difference, it seemed, and he supposed he had Lemon Girl to thank.

"This is Big Sparky," he said to her later, feeling he owed her something and remembering she had wanted him to show her more things.

She shifted the baseball bat around in her hands. "What do you do with this?"

"When I was younger, I played baseball, and this was sort of like my good luck charm."

"Baseball," she said thoughtfully, and nodded. "I saw that a couple of times on TV, but I didn't get it. That's still great, Morty. Were you on TV?"

"No," Morty said. "I was just a kid playing baseball in Little League. I guess I was pretty good at it back then. My grandparents came to every game."

He showed her a picture on the wall, one of his grandparents. She studied it.

"Where are they?" she asked.

"They aren't around anymore," he said.

"Why not?"

Morty sighed. "I don't feel like going into it right now. That's the best way I can explain it. No one lives forever. They're gone, but they left me that bottle of water I showed you, and they left me all that land where you and the other girls were born."

"Have you thought about making more orchard girls?"

"No way!" Morty exclaimed. "You three are plenty enough. More than enough. But at least you've been helping with everything, Lemon Girl, and shown me that I can count on you."

With a large smile, she pressed her body against his. "Aw, thank you, Morty!"

Later that night, Morty slept soundly. It didn't last. Neither did the peace that had settled in his house for the past day.

The shatter of glass woke him. He sat up. He heard the noisy orchard girls carrying on as they had before, but it was different this time, angry, and the orange girls weren't the only ones.

Lemon Girl's voice shrieked above the rest.

"What happened now?" he grumbled and pushed out of the bedroom toward the living room.

"It's your fault!" Lemon Girl shouted at the orange girls.

"It's yours, too," one replied, brushing orange hair from her eyes.

Morty's eyes fixed on what remained of the glass bottle, broken pieces littered across the carpet. The bottle had been broken, and his living room carpet was wet with the water of life.

He stared, his mouth open. One of the orange girls sniffled.

"We're sorry," she said. Morty faced the girls, trembling with growing anger. Lemon Girl swallowed. The orange girls backed away.

"She told us about the water!" one of the orange girls erupted. She pointed at Lemon Girl.

"I didn't tell you to break it!" she fired back.

"You told us about what it could do," the orange girl said. "We wondered, since it created us, if we could use it to create orchard boys."

"You don't know how it works!" Lemon Girl said to her. "You would create more orchard girls and Morty doesn't want any more orchard girls! Tell them, Morty!"

"All of you need to go," Morty told them. "Right now."

"But—"

"Go! Leave me alone! All of you!" He charged. They streaked out the door in fear. He slammed it behind them and screamed.

He fell onto the couch. That magical liquid, gone—and over something so stupid. Did those girls not have a bit of sense in their heads? He dropped his head into his hands, seething with anger, and worked on taking slow, controlled breaths to calm himself. He didn't even notice the absence of Big Sparky, its usual corner empty.

He didn't realize until after that meek knock on the door, and after answering it, that Lemon Girl had taken Big Sparky with her. She walked in and stood within the front door, holding the bat in both hands. The aluminum glistened with juice, traces of orange pulp sticking to it.

"It's just me," Lemon Girl said. "By myself."

Morty's anger diminished to a dull confusion. "What happened?" he asked, his eyes on the bat.

"I'm sorry about what they did," Lemon Girl said. "I took care of them. It will never happen again."

"But the water of life," Morty said. "It's—wait. You said you did *what?*"

"They aren't around anymore."

"Do you mean you *killed* them?" He stared at Big Sparky. "With my bat?"

Lemon Girl let out a sigh. "You didn't really like them that much anyway, did you? You liked me the best, I knew that, and those girls were always jealous. That's why they wanted to use the water to make orchard boys for themselves. They wanted what we had, Morty. But do you really want to know why I didn't want them to try it?"

She stepped closer to him. "Because I thought, 'what if another lemon girl is born?' I couldn't stand the thought of that. I've always been the only one. I've always been special to you. Isn't that right?"

Morty shook his head. She was so far from human. The girl was the product of a fruit tree.

She had lived for weeks and couldn't have developed on a mental or an emotional level in such a small period of time. She had no grasp of right and wrong. You couldn't just kill anyone who disagreed with you—well, you *shouldn't* at least, Morty thought.

"You really don't understand, do you?" Morty asked her.

"What don't I understand?"

"You just don't. Go."

"You want me to go, too?"

"And leave the bat." Morty reached out to take it from her. She held it, defiant. He tensed at her resistance, but yanked it away.

She stood with hurt in her eyes. "I don't know what to do," she whispered. "I can't make it on my own. You know that." She bit her quivering yellow lip. "Don't do this to me."

Morty walked away. He heard the choked sob, far behind him. "Please!"

With Big Sparky in his hand, he kept walking. Her shrill scream jabbed into his eardrums. The rapid motion of footsteps came next, Lemon Girl running at him, and he turned too late to see the large fruit bowl in her hands right before she smashed it against his head. Pain erupted in his temple. His vision flashed. He collapsed onto the carpet. In the distance, a door slammed.

Wetness trickled down his face, blood. Weakness overcame him. He almost fainted. His head swam. He stretched an arm out. A short span away, he felt the damp carpet.

He rubbed his hand against the carpet and moistened his fingers with the water of life. He massaged the water into his bleeding temple.

He repeated the action several times, working what he could of the water into his injury. Bit by bit, the pain began to alleviate. His vision cleared. He regained his wits. A throbbing soreness remained, but that was all, though the water had worked its last miracle for him.

He saw Big Sparky on the floor nearby. He picked it up, stood, and walked to the front door. When he opened it, he saw she hadn't wandered far from the house. A ripple of mounting fury entered him. His grip on the bat tightened. Teeth clenched, Morty walked out the door after her. He followed her from the grass of his property, where he saw the bodies of the orange girls strewn, to the road.

The yellow girl turned and saw him. Her eyes widened. She ran. Morty chased, gained on her, and swung Big Sparky with both hands. The aluminum bat split her head wide open. Lemon pulp, seeds, and juice splorched across the street.

Morty stared down at the sprawled body of Lemon Girl and the juice running from her. The anger drained from him. An uneasy feeling settled in its place. Morty laid Big Sparky on the ground and lifted the body.

With numbness in his chest, he carried her to the back of his truck, repeating dubious reassurances to himself all the way.

"She attacked me. She killed the other girls. She might have killed me. I did what I had to do. It isn't murder if she isn't human, right? She grew from a tree. Real people don't grow from trees."

He set her in the cab. He followed suit with each of the orange girls. He took his keys and a shovel and drove back out to the orchard to bury them.

There were no more orchard girls, only an abundance of large oranges and lemons heaped around the silent trees.

Morty pulled the shovel from the back of his truck. Surrounded by piles of citrus fruit, he began to dig.

The Dead of December

I: The Coldest December

Abbie walked. Her limbs ached. Her fingers were numb. Her hair glittered crystalline with ice and snow. Her face, etched by the trials of the past, might easily be mistaken for that of a woman's and not a girl's, though she was but fifteen years of age.

How cold it was. She could feel it numbing her extremities, but beneath the numbness raged a deeply burrowed pain she could best imagine as invisible screws of ice driven through her joints and bones.

She struggled to hold her eyes open. If she closed them, she feared, they might freeze shut. As it was, thin layers of snow coated her eyelashes. Each time she blinked, a pinch of snow dropped from them.

Constricted by the frozen December night, it became more difficult for Abbie to remain awake, but she defied every urge to drop into the soft white blanket and close her eyes to sleep an eternity.

Thick snow kept pelting down. She reasserted her effort to keep her eyes open, pushed her thoughts as far from the reality of this night as she was able, and reached through her gloom of memories for the memory of the fire.

It bellowed from a burning metal drum, smoking, reeking, but it warmed her, melted the ice away, and countered the coldness.

She remembered the steaming cup of broth between her hands, warming them while the seasoned golden liquid warmed her throat. She imagined its nourishment spreading into her body.

The pot of broth was one of the best meals Abbie could remember, but it had not lasted long.

On most days, she could only hope to come by a stale crust of bread or a handful of wild berries. In these past days, neither had been available. This winter was cruel like no other.

What had kept her alive through the last weeks? Was it her will to survive or her inherent sense of danger?

The latter had saved her from those jackals in the snow. The large man in brown fur, an image of broken yellowed teeth, bloodshot eyes, ravenous hunger, and butchery, silent and eager, had smiled to her in passing. She had recognized the intentions beneath it and kept her distance from the man, a wise decision.

He kept company with two others, and the three of them, all in warm fur, worked steadily at a form in the snow. When Abbie fled, the three men returned to their meal. She heard the cry in her hurrying steps of escape and her freezing heart nearly cracked.

"No, please," emerged the boy's wracked final plea.

Abbie shivered, returning from her icy trance to the present. She stared across seemingly endless whiteness and pushed each foot ahead of the other.

One step meant an arduous process, never mind the next. Stabs of coldness and increasing difficulty slowed her progress across the white field.

What is that? She strained to look ahead through the falling snow.

A small, dark shape, a square, appeared to her through the constant whiteness. A house? Out here, in the middle of the icy plain, a house? Surely it was an illusion of her troubled wasting mind, Abbie first supposed, but then she saw the clouds of smoke puffing from its chimney.

Abbie found a new driving force in her steps. She forced herself onward, defying the cold. She had to keep walking. The harsher the toll of winter became, the more she fought with every step to reach the house. Finally, somehow, she arrived.

She stumbled to its door, grabbed the handle, and tried to open it in vain. She slumped against it and beat her numb hands against the wooden surface.

"Help me," Abbie called in a frigid, cracked voice. Her own voice reminded her of that dying boy's desperate cries in the snow. This ignited a renewed pounding against the door.

She sank into the snow, but then the door opened. A trace of warmth touched her. She raised her head and saw a figure standing there.

"A girl!" the gray-haired woman exclaimed. She limped outside with the assistance of a hooked cane.

She slipped her cane under one arm and struggled to pull the girl up. Abbie pushed what strength she could muster into her rubbery legs to assist, and between their combined efforts, she came to her feet. The woman guided her into the warm shelter of the house.

Soon, Abbie stretched on a brown rug in front of a burning fireplace with a blanket draped over her. The woman shut the front door and sealed the cold away.

Abbie's teeth still chattered. The cold had yet to expire from her senses. Even the heat from the fireplace could not drive it away quickly enough to satisfy her freezing body.

The woman rested against her cane and looked down at her. "Poor girl," she said. "Look at you. You are half-frozen from the cold! I'll put on a pot of tea."

The woman disappeared through a doorway into what must have been the home's kitchen, because she returned with a kettle, which, with the use of an iron poker, she extended into the fireplace and brought to rest over the orange-red heat.

"The oven is out," the woman explained while the tea brewed in the fireplace, "but we have blankets and a good fire." She paused, and her tone softened. "Forgive me. I am Annette, Annette Mender. Please tell me, girl, what is your name and where do you come from?"

"Abbie," the girl answered once she could hold the teeth-chattering to a minimum. "I came from—it's a bad place."

"A bad place, you say? Are you from the Western Fringes?"

"What?"

Annette shook her head. "Never mind. Just lie there and try to warm up. Are you hungry?"

"Yes," Abbie said.

"I'll put on some soup for you."

Abbie attempted a reply but managed only a slight nod. Annette offered a gracious smile before ambling back into the kitchen. Soon she placed a covered pot of liquid into the fireplace in the same fashion as she had with the tea kettle.

Abbie's eyes wandered over the interior of the house. Its adornments were tasteful if antiquated.

Her gaze stopped on a framed picture against one wall, a picture of a couple. Abbie identified Annette as the woman in the picture, but she was many years younger, the gray absent from her hair and the wrinkles gone from her glowing skin.

"I was married, years ago," Annette spoke, seeing Abbie's attention focused on the picture.

Abbie took a breath and managed to speak. "Not anymore?"

"He was taken from me, many years ago."

"I'm—I'm sorry."

"He left one day for the hunt," Annette said, "but after that day, he never came back. In the fields I found his old brass lighter. I still have it." She sighed, looked at the picture on the wall, and down to her lap, where her hands rested. She rubbed them together.

"He went too close to the Western Fringes, I believe," Annette murmured.

"What are the Western Fringes?" Abbie asked, remembering Annette's previous mention of this.

"The Western Fringes—a frightening place, full of thieves, murderers, and scavengers, so it is said."

"Although," Annette added after a few further seconds of reflection, "there are perhaps worse things." A touch of concern entered her features. "I don't mean to frighten you."

"No, it's all right," Abbie said. How could mere words cause any more damage than a life spent in the place itself? Abbie now recognized the place Annette called the Western Fringes. She had lived there all of her life.

She dispelled the memories and looked around the cozy house again, finding comfort until she saw the heavy black door in the far corner with its chain and thick padlock. She stared at it for a while before turning her eyes back to Annette.

"You have a nice home," Abbie said to her.

Annette smiled. The kettle whistled. "Tea's ready," she said.

II: Jackals in the Snow

The three pushed through the thick snow, hungry, and nothing, not even the cold, could overpower their hunger. When fresh meat was at stake, those who faltered starved.

Jarvis walked beside and just ahead of Marco, who walked in a daze of gradually slowing footsteps. Broderick's steps tailed a short distance behind Marco's. That is, until Broderick raised the thick leg bone and swung it full-force into the back of Marco's head.

Marco toppled into the snow. Jarvis spun around and tensed, his arms poised to defend himself against the larger man, but Broderick's attention landed on the wasting body of the man who now gushed red into white.

"He was slowing us down," Broderick justified. He lowered the bloody end of the bludgeoning bone into his other hand. Red wetness, not yet frozen, rubbed into his palm. With the large bone in his hands, he watched Jarvis.

Jarvis looked back at him. It was not a direct challenge, he deemed after the silent combat of wills, but a fierce declaration of Broderick's intention to survive, even if Jarvis should come at him this very second. Jarvis allowed his eyes to slip downward to the body of Marco. The thin man had been the weakest of them all, he decided. Broderick was right. He had only obeyed his deepest desires, those that again fueled Jarvis while he watched their meal bleed in the snow.

Broderick wanted to eat. So did Jarvis.

"Well then," Jarvis said, dropping his defensive posture, "no reason we ought to let the meat go to waste, right?"

Broderick lowered his bone club. The two of them set about butchering Marco in a quick and coarse fashion. Broderick produced a sharp-edged piece of bone which worked well for the task. They ate their fill of the raw human meat.

Even as he ate, Jarvis decided it would never be a smart decision to turn his back to Broderick.

For the continuation of their journey across the fields of snow and ice, Jarvis walked to one side of Broderick but maintained a healthy distance, and at all times, kept an eye on the large, wild-haired man who lumbered closely in match with his own steps.

On this freezing December day, Jarvis found no remorse for Marco. He had felt a twinge of anxiety the moment Broderick took him down, but not a concern for his fellow man. It was concern for his own well-being. When survival was the priority, Jarvis thought, that was the way it should be.

Besides, Marco could not have claimed innocence of such deeds. When Jarvis and Broderick first found the man in that cave, he had hunched drooling over a rusted pot of boiling water and the tender flesh of a girl who cooked inside.

Broderick grunted. Jarvis shot a glance over.

"What?" he asked. Broderick pointed ahead. Jarvis looked but kept Broderick's position in his peripheral vision. Ahead, through the relentless snow, Jarvis saw only more snow.

He shook his head. Broderick grunted and, with emphasis, stabbed a finger in the same direction. Jarvis stared toward the area for a while longer until at last he saw the house. He released a frosty breath of acknowledgment.

A house meant food, both men knew, especially when the interior appeared to be lit. The smoke from its chimney meant there would be warmth inside.

Jarvis thought he saw the hint of footprints earlier, but the constant blanketing snowfall made it difficult to be certain. Had Broderick known? He had carried them in this direction for minutes, but spoke little.

Jarvis quickened his movements to keep up with the larger man. They moved for the snow-covered house.

Inside the warm house, Annette Mender struck the brass lighter and held its flame to the bowl of her pipe. She puffed clouds of fragrant smoke. Despite its pleasantness, it proved intense. Abbie coughed from where she sat near the fireplace.

"I'm sorry, dear," Annette apologized. "I'll go into the kitchen."

"It's all right," Abbie said. "I'm just not used to it." She found she enjoyed the older woman's company, whether smoking or not.

"You've had an awful time getting here, I can understand," Annette said. "That's enough to deal with without having to suffer through an old woman's nasty habits."

"Is that the lighter?" Abbie said, changing the conversation.

Annette glanced to the shiny lighter in her gnarled hand. It appeared to glimmer.

"It was my husband's, yes," Annette said, "if that is what you mean." She studied the lighter, becoming immersed in her thoughts, and Abbie's attention drifted toward the black door again.

She wanted to ask, but did not. Somehow, mentioning the door seemed inappropriate. She didn't know why. It seemed out of place here, like some ugly mold infestation within the kind woman's otherwise warm home. Before Abbie could further ponder it, a sharp knock interrupted her thoughts.

Annette glanced up from her pipe. "More company?" she murmured. She chewed the pipe's stem and looked to Abbie. Finally, she stood and shifted toward the door. She placed a hand on the door's knob, unlatched the deadbolt, and opened the door.

"Pardon me, miss," Jarvis ejected through a hiss of reeking icy breath. "It's cold out here." The man rubbed his arms together in a mild effort to warm himself.

Abbie's hands squeezed the blanket she held close. She could not see the man from where she sat, but the familiar sense of danger spiked. Her heartbeat heaved into a panicked chug. She stood and the blanket slipped from her hands.

Jarvis's eyes caught the motion. He looked past Annette toward Abbie, who backed against the wall. The two stared at one another. Another familiar figure, much larger than Jarvis, moved into the front doorway.

"Hello, girlie," Broderick said to Abbie.

Abbie gasped. Fear clamored in her ears.

Puzzled, Annette looked toward Abbie, and the moment she turned, Broderick grabbed her by the throat.

She cried out, startled. Her surprise became fear. Broderick squeezed her throat and choked her attempted scream to a gurgle. Her pipe fell to the floor.

Jarvis moved past, straight toward Abbie, but she was ready. She grabbed the kettle from the hearth, and even while it burned her skin, she flung hot tea across Jarvis's legs. He bellowed. Abbie threw the teapot. He ducked, but not quickly enough. The flying teapot struck him in the head. Abbie rushed wide of him, her rapid steps propelling her for the kitchen.

Broderick threw Annette to the floor and charged after the girl. Abbie reached the kitchen doorway, Broderick behind her. His arm caught her around the neck. He pulled her backward. She lost her balance, flailing back into Broderick's arms.

Broderick clamped a large, powerful hand against the side of her head, and whispered, with no uncertainty, "Hold still or I'll snap your neck!"

Jarvis skirted around them, into the kitchen. Broderick's thin, grimy accomplice stopped at the kitchen counter. He threw open drawers, some of them coming free and hitting the floor. Their varied contents spilled across the floor.

From one of the drawers, he snatched out a large kitchen knife. He turned to approach Abbie, who remained locked in Broderick's grip, and held the blade against her throat.

"I should slice you open right here for what you did to me," he said to her with a gust of foul breath that brought nausea to her choked senses.

"Not yet," Broderick said. "What about that old hag? Where is she?"

"In the next room," Jarvis said, and with a cruel little laugh, added, "Knocked out cold!" He looked around to study the kitchen. "Looks like we've got plenty of food here. I'm starving!"

Broderick grunted his assent. He dragged Abbie back into the living area. Abbie strained while struggling to breathe. Black swirled through her vision.

Jarvis pulled Annette up from the floor. She awakened to a half-conscious state, on the brink of swooning. Jarvis seized her and positioned the knife against her throat.

Abbie renewed her struggling despite her lack of strength or wits. Broderick shook her, a harsh motion that did nothing to stop her continued efforts, useless as they were.

From not far away, Jarvis chuckled. He pressed the cold blade against Annette's skin. "Should I just kill her and get it over with?"

"No," Broderick said. "Not yet."

Jarvis's eyebrows came together, not quite understanding, but he waited.

Broderick continued to restrain Abbie, a simple task for the near-giant, but there was something here which, despite his constant hunger, had captured his attention more keenly than the food in the kitchen and their two captives—the black door, chained and padlocked.

"What's in there?" he asked Annette.

"The basement," she answered.

"What's in the basement?"

"Nothing," she said.

Broderick and Jarvis traded glances. "Where's the key?" Broderick asked.

Annette didn't answer. Jarvis pushed the knife's blade into her soft skin, just a bit, and shifted it enough to part the flesh and release a trickle of blood down her neck. She gasped.

"Where's the key?" Broderick repeated. "If you don't tell us, we'll kill you and the girl. We'll kill you both and we'll tear this place apart until we find it. We'll have the key whether you live or die and it makes no difference to me which!"

"That door," Annette said to Broderick and Jarvis, "should never be opened."

Jarvis flung her to the floor and kicked her in the ribs while Abbie again fought Broderick's grip.

Jarvis stooped over to dig through Annette's pockets. He came out with the brass lighter, which he studied briefly before pocketing. He went into Annette's pockets again until he found an iron ring yielding numerous keys.

"What do we have here?" he asked. He stepped back from Annette's prone form and held the keys up for Broderick to see. "Let's see if one of them works, shall we?"

Jarvis left Annette on the floor and went to the black door. He looked over the door, and with one hand, took the chain that stretched across it. He pursued its length to the center of the door where the padlock secured the chain's ends together.

Jarvis pushed the first of several keys into the lock. The first selection failed to open it. He tried another with the same results. He went through the rest of the keys in turn until he reached the final key, which also failed to work at first, but he jiggled the key for a moment longer and the lock popped open. The chain fell with a series of clinks into a metallic pile at the base of the door.

"That's it," Jarvis said.

"Wait," Annette said, and made an attempt to pull herself up. Jarvis crossed over to her and delivered another kick which put her back to the floor.

Abbie moved again in an attempt to free herself. Broderick flung her face-first against the door. She cried out with the stunning impact and collapsed. Broderick hoisted her aside and stepped in front of the door to open it.

A deep creaking sounded through the blackness within. A set of steps led downward into the dark.

"We've got it open," Jarvis said. "Should we just kill them now?"

"Let's see what's down there, first."

It was clear Jarvis didn't like this idea, but he didn't argue. Broderick lifted Abbie and made a careful descent, hauling the girl down the steps into the basement with Jarvis half-dragging Annette right behind.

III: The Dark Well

Abbie's instincts became her terror. What she felt in the darkness of the basement gripped her heart, seized her muscles, and filled her with terror.

Although Broderick's arms remained around her, he no longer pressed on her throat with the same crushing force of before. Jarvis struck a flame in the dark. The illumination from the brass lighter spread thinly across the basement.

The instant Abbie saw the open pit in the middle of the stone floor, she knew it to be the source of all she felt. From it exuded unrest, grief, and deeper into its depths, absolute hatred.

When Broderick walked past it, Abbie forced herself to look into the pit. She could see no bottom to it.

"What's this?" Jarvis called. He rummaged through some boxes against the back basement wall.

Suddenly, the lighter's flame went out. The room went black. Jarvis again struck the lighter and the pit that might have been a shaft to the center of the world returned to visibility.

Jarvis muttered at the worthless items in the boxes, old clothes and scraps of newspaper, which he tossed aside.

"Nothing but garbage in here," he said.

Annette lay on the cold basement floor near the bottom of the steps. One side of her face was bruised purple and black.

When she stirred, everyone's attention shifted to her miserable attempts to gather herself up.

Jarvis threw an armful of clothes back into one of the boxes and stood. "I'm tired of this. We're wasting our time down here. I'm hungry."

"Then go eat," Broderick said.

"I believe I will," Jarvis said. "If there's anything down here that'll be of use to us, it can wait till later."

"Don't forget about that one," Broderick said, nodding toward Annette. "I'm not watching both of them."

Jarvis walked over to Annette, his knife in his hand.

"There's nothing down here," Jarvis fired at her. "Why did you waste our time with this? I haven't had a meal in ages! You've got *food* upstairs and there's nothing down here but trash!" He yanked her to her feet only to shove her back to the floor.

"Get up!" he ordered her, despite having just shoved her down. When she failed to respond, he dragged her up and pushed her toward the pit.

Through the basement's oppressive blackness, Abbie found the strength to squirm again in desperation, because she knew what would soon happen. She knew she had to do anything she could to prevent it.

Jarvis gave Annette a fierce shove toward the pit. She stumbled and caught herself, swaying. Abbie's heart raced. She kept struggling, unable to free herself, but managed to reposition herself and threw herself into a desperate act that would free her or result in her death.

Across the basement, Jarvis shouted at Annette's back, something unintelligible but full of malice, right before he planted a boot hard into her backside and sent her over the edge of the pit.

With her face near Broderick's wrist, Abbie bit deep. The large man howled and snatched his hand away. Flesh came away in Abbie's teeth.

She escaped Broderick's grip and scrambled back from him. Blood ran from the back of his hand. He stood in momentary disbelief.

At that moment, Abbie saw Jarvis standing at the edge of the pit, and Annette Mender, the kind old woman who had saved

Abbie, showing her a warmth she had never before known, was gone. Numbness filled Abbie's stomach.

Broderick clenched his bloody hand into a fist. Fury darkened his face into murder. He stalked toward Abbie. She took her eyes from the pit and rose to her feet, heedless of pain, internal and external. She faced the towering man.

"You shouldn't have done that," Broderick said to her, his voice low. In the barest trickle of light from the brass lighter's flame, the blood covering the back of his fist glistened black. Droplets fell in a quiet rhythm to the gray stone floor.

A distant sound, high-pitched and unpleasant, sounded. From near the pit, Jarvis cocked his head, listening, bewildered.

"Now, girlie," Broderick said to Abbie, coming toward her, "you're going to *suffer.*"

She kicked him between the legs as hard as she could. He gasped and dropped to his knees. Abbie dashed past him for the basement stairs.

Jarvis, the flame of the brass lighter shining golden on his features, ran to intercept her. She ducked beneath his arms and plowed into his stomach. He wheezed, surprised when she knocked the air from him, and fell aside. The lighter's flame flickered out and everything went black.

The once-distant wailing came closer, increasing in volume, erupting into a mad shriek. Visible by some pale phantom illumination, it screamed from the pit with an accompanying gust of asphyxiating heat.

Jarvis shouted and clutched at his ears, but his eardrums had already erupted. Blood ran from his ears. The thing that shot from the pit latched onto him, screeching and ripping at his eyes with long, sharp nails.

Blood ran from his eyes and ears and the thing kept screeching, tearing the flesh from his face and throat, and with incredible power, it hurled his body through the air. Jarvis struck the far basement wall with a crack. The impact broke almost every bone in his body.

It crossed the basement in the span of a second to seize Jarvis's head with leathery hands and slam his skull into the stone floor again and again. Jarvis's death left a stain on the basement floor.

Broderick saw it turn upon him. He came to his feet with his hands over his ears. The features, once Annette Mender's, had withered and warped. Her clothing hung in tatters.

This was not the old woman anymore. It was the product of a place or a force worse than anything Broderick had ever known in the Western Fringes.

Broderick ran for the basement's stairs. Her—its—toothless mouth stretched wide. It catapulted through the air and caught him at the base of the steps.

From the black door, Abbie burst into the living area of the house. She ran across the room and out through the house's front door, back into the cold. She heard the screeching and the screams, sounds which cut deeper than this December's cold ever could. She fled into the whiteness, her only escape, with no idea of the thing ripping the flesh from Broderick's bones in the basement of the house.

The black door exploded from its hinges. The rug burned. Smoke rose from the furniture. When it emerged from the house's front door and surged across the white snow, melting all in its path, the house burned.

In the basement where the dark well had released the courier of death, the blood of Broderick's torturous final moments ran down the basement steps.

Across the snow, Abbie moved east, pushing away from the house that burned well behind her. She didn't look back.

The snow from above nestled in her hair and stung her skin. Abbie's hand closed around the cold brass lighter taken from Jarvis in her last-minute escape from the basement. She closed her eyes. Tears fell. She raised a shaking hand to sweep them away before they froze to her cheeks.

* * *

It moved through the air over the snowy ground and crossed the fields of white, leaving a wide path of melted snow. It moved west.

Among the few scattered dead trees which stood on the snowy waste of the Western Fringes, the last survivors raised their weary heads. They saw the infernal rage coming from the east. When it reached them, they went without a struggle into the December night.

* * *

Abbie trudged through the snow, exhausted. The wind whistled over the snow and ice to jab through her lethargy. It roused strange, distant thoughts within her.

She was no stranger to pain. To survive, she had to face it, and so she did. Surrender had never been in her fiery blood.

The colorful cluster of lights far ahead, greens and reds, lent her a forlorn brand of hope, even if such a hope might be false and the lights were a mirage in the coldness that clenched her muscles and bones and dulled her mind.

Among the greens and reds, she began to distinguish white lights. Strings of them lined snow-covered buildings, she could see in time, evoking sparkles from the numerous icicles dangling from the edges of rooftops.

When she reached the edge of town, she saw no one on the streets. She walked along a snow-blanketed street and turned up a separate, narrower street which branched from it. When she passed a building with windows, she stopped to peer in. It was dark inside.

No matter, she thought. It must be warmer inside there than it is out here.

She found a snow-covered loose brick near the building's outer wall, took it into ice-numbed fingers, and smashed it through the glass. She knocked away each remaining shard of glass until the window was clear. She heaved, muscles burning, to climb in through the window. Once inside the dark building's interior, she collapsed to the floor.

She lay there for an indeterminable span, hungry and exhausted, but at least protected by some shelter from the cold, though a portion of it continued to leak through the broken window. When she felt her digits tingling, free in part from the cold, she struggled toward a wall and fell against it.

The cold from the window sliced her again. She shivered, pulled out the brass lighter, and struck it.

A meek, wavering flame came from the lighter. She held it close until she could feel its warmth. When it went out, she struck it again.

In this empty sanctuary, she had naught but the brass lighter and the clothes she wore, but she endured.

She laid her head against the wall, closed her eyes, and tried her best to find sleep. In her fifteen years, Abbie had never been so tired.

The snow kept falling. The lights went dark.

Wreckage

He was left in the dark with no vehicle, no working telephone to be found, and no one in sight until the headlights broke the darkness, magnifying and almost blinding him.

The yellow cab ground to a stop on the shoulder. Before rolling the window down, its driver looked back at the flashers of an abandoned vehicle blinking farther up the road.

"Is that you back there?" the cabbie asked the man on the side of the road.

"It was," the man said.

"What happened?"

"It died and wouldn't restart. I'll have to call a tow truck to pick it up."

"I know a guy."

"It's all right. I'll worry about it later. Can you get me home?"

"Sure thing, buddy."

The walking man climbed into the back of the cab. The cab driver's eyes focused on him through the rear-view mirror.

"Where to?" the cabbie asked.

The man gave his address. The cabbie nodded, shifted gears, and began driving.

The man in the back settled against the seat. Any minor comfort he might have achieved within the next minutes jolted from his reach when the cab suddenly braked.

Red lights were ahead. They lined the street for quite a distance. Somewhere among them, blue lights flashed and the red-and-white lights of an ambulance spun.

"It looks like an accident," the cabbie said.

The passenger took in the red lights and the long line of vehicles ahead.

"I guess we're in for a wait," he sighed.

The cab slowed to a halt. When the car in front of them began to move, the taxi again rolled forward.

They came closer to the lights surrounding the scene of the accident. When they passed near, both men looked out and had to squint against the lights.

The cabbie drew a soft breath. "This is a bad one."

He turned forward again to watch the road. The man in the back continued to look out, absorbing the scene of destruction.

Through the glaring lights, he could see the warped, wrenched remains of human and machine driven into asphalt and dust. Broken metal and glass covered the street, the intersecting train tracks, and the ground beyond. Farther out, the darkened behemoth of a train sat silent on the tracks.

The smell of exhaust was strong here. The man caught another smell, a deep, earthy smokiness, within it.

The traffic thinned. The cab accelerated.

The smell lingered. So did the image of the destroyed vehicle, unrecognizable as anything but smashed bloody and blackened pieces, remnants of lives burned away into ash and smoke.

He tried to forget, pushing his thoughts along another course, but found that he could not; as if tainted by the horrid smell and sight of the wreckage, he could only pretend to ignore it, but he could not deny the images haunting him or the feeling deep in his stomach. He felt sick.

The cabbie looked at him through the rear-view mirror. "Are you all right, buddy?" he asked.

The man gave a quick nod, more of a dismissal than a truthful answer. He sat without speaking for the rest of the ride and soon stared downward because he could not seem to look at anything in quite the same fashion.

The cab turned into a modest residential area. The slow ride drifted along the street past several houses before coming to an eventual stop at a quiet suburban corner.

"This is it," the cabbie said.

"How much do I owe you?" the passenger asked.

"Twenty-four dollars and seventy-five cents," the cabbie said.

The man in the back seat checked his wallet. He had twenty-five dollars. He paid the cabbie. This left him with a single remaining shiny twenty-five cent piece.

He climbed out of the cab. Of the visible neighborhood, the only windows lit were those of his own home.

"Have a good night, buddy," the cabbie said. He smiled, too broadly.

The taxi cab drove away. The man walked toward his home, where his family waited within, their eyes full of smoke in a house with walls that seemed as glass.

When he embraced his wife and children and held them close, even they could sense it, even if they could not speak of it or realize the change which hung upon the man's thoughts on this night, that which loomed unseen and might, at any moment in time with a touch, a whisper, or a breath, dash the glass walls into a million pieces of chaos.

Acknowledgments

My first and foremost words of gratitude are for Carrie, for her invaluable support and for being herself.

My thanks to the friends and family who have remained supportive despite our being scattered out across this ball of rock, water, and air we call the earth.

Thanks are also due to the publishers, editors, artists, and authors I have worked with over these past years and to all of the readers who have supported what I do along the way.

It wasn't always an easy road, but it was a better one for you. Until the next.

About the Author

Tommy B. Smith is a writer of dark fiction, author of *The Mourner's Cradle* and *Poisonous,* as well as works appearing in numerous magazines and anthologies throughout the years. His presence currently infests Fort Smith, Arkansas, where he resides with his wife and cats.

More information can be found on his website at http://tommybsmith.net.

www.ingramcontent.com/pod-product-compliance
Lightning Source LLC
Chambersburg PA
CBHW070602180626
46817CB00005B/1952